Wind Dancer

CHRIS PLATT

Wind Dancer

PEACHTREE
ATLANTA

Published by
PEACHTREE PUBLISHERS
1700 Chattahoochee Avenue
Atlanta, Georgia 30318-2112
www.peachtree-online.com

Cover design by Nicola Carmack
Interior composition by Melanie McMahon Ives

Printed in February 2014 by RR Donnelley & Sons in Harrisonburg, Virginia, in the United States of America
10 9 8 7 6 5 4 3 2 1
First Edition

Library of Congress Cataloging-in-Publication Data

Platt, Chris, 1959-
 Wind dancer / Chris Platt.
    pages cm
 Summary: Having lost her beloved pony in a traumatic accident, thirteen-year-old Ali is reluctant to help her parents care for a neglected, malnourished Appaloosa, but working with Wind Dancer is a good distraction from problems surrounding her brother, who recently returned from Afghanistan with a missing leg and PTSD.
  ISBN: 978-1-56145-736-6
 [1. Family problems—Fiction. 2. Post-traumatic stress disorder—Fiction. 3. Amputees—Fiction. 4. Veterans—Fiction. 5. Appaloosa horse—Fiction. 6. Horses—Fiction. 7. Brothers and sisters—Fiction.] I. Title.
 PZ7.P7123115Wm 2014
 [Fic]—dc23
                  2013026283

This is for the men and women of our armed forces, who fight for our freedom and make great sacrifices.

And to their families, who love them and keep the home fires burning.

—C. P.

One

Something's wrong." Ali flattened her nose against the school bus window, trying to catch sight of the horses. "Can you see them?" Cara asked.

Ali craned her neck, peering into the dilapidated barn at the rear of the large corner lot. It was none of her business. But the image of the skinny horses she'd last seen a week ago remained. They'd left hoofprints in her memory.

Maybe someone else would help them.

Cara's mom had already called Animal Control several weeks ago, but the only thing the officer did was examine the horses and talk to Mrs. Marshall about how to care for them.

Ali had to snort at that one. Apparently mistreated animals couldn't be taken away from their owner right away. Several inspections to document progress—or the lack thereof—were required before anything could be done. She felt sick, thinking of the horses going hungry while everyone waited for proper procedure to be followed.

Ali's mother had tried going straight to the horses' owner. Shortly after the investigation, she'd taken a tuna casserole to Mrs. Marshall, in hopes she'd get invited in and could assess the situation. But Mrs. M just grabbed the casserole, told her mother to mind her own business, and slammed the door in her face.

Now Ali eyed the Marshall property. Here on the edge of the high mountain desert, water was in limited supply and most people didn't have much of a lawn. Mrs. M's grass was dead, dead, dead, never to rise again. She was growing a great crop of tumbleweeds and goatheads instead.

As the bus stopped to let off one of the other kids, Ali studied Mrs. Marshall's small, tan house. The paint on the siding was chipped and the porch was rickety. Had something happened to the elderly woman so she couldn't take care of things anymore? Didn't old people fall down and break hips, or something?

"Have you seen Mrs. Marshall lately?" she asked Cara.

"Nope." Cara pulled her backpack onto her lap and zipped her cell phone into the front pocket. "The neighbor kid told me she wigged out and threw rocks at the paperboy a few days ago. His mom tried to contact Mrs. Marshall's son, but they haven't heard back."

Ali tucked a strand of her long dark hair behind her ear and looked at the barn again. She didn't want to care. *But what if something* had *happened to the old woman and her horses?*

"Trade me places." Cara climbed over Ali and squished in next to the window. "I'm taller than you. Maybe I can see them."

Ali scooted over. "Maybe she locked the horses in the barn so she can feed them and fatten them up?" she said hopefully. But she knew in her gut that probably wasn't true. Most likely the horses were kept out of sight so the neighbors wouldn't report her again. "Mrs. Marshall seemed awfully upset that other people were getting involved. She was pretty mean to my mom."

"Those horses might be better off if someone just set them free," Cara said.

Ali wasn't so sure. She stared out the window at the northern Nevada landscape as the bus pulled onto the road. The ground was covered in sand and sagebrush as far as the eye could see. A few pinyon pines sprouted here and there; patches of sparse desert grass grew between them. The wild mustang herds that roamed the desert had trouble surviving on such meager forage. How would a domestic horse fare?

The bus slowed, pulled onto the gravel shoulder, and stopped in a cloud of dust. Ali stood quickly, trying to shake the sad thoughts of the horses from her mind, and her foot landed squarely on someone else's. She glanced up into the blue eyes of the local veterinarian's son. His toes squished beneath her shoe before she jumped back. Ali felt her cheeks flush. She opened her mouth to apologize, but the words stuck in her throat. She backed up and let him go first, forcing Cara to wait until he was totally off the bus before they made their way down the aisle.

"Way to go, McCormick." Cara poked her in the back. "That's one way of getting his attention. But it might have been easier just to say hi."

Ali's cheeks grew even hotter. She didn't want Jamie Forrester's attention. He had been there with his dad after the accident, something she didn't need reminding of, ever. Thankfully he hardly ever rode the bus.

Ali and Cara stepped off the bus and into the warm afternoon sun. Jamie was way ahead of them, striding purposefully down the road. At school he hung out with some of the city kids, but his T-shirt, jeans, and well-worn boots screamed country boy.

"Want to come over tonight?" Cara hefted her backpack onto her shoulder. "My mom's grilling hamburgers."

Ali's stomach growled. Cara's mom could do wonders with

that grill. "Sounds good, but I can't. We've only got a few days of school left before summer, and I've got a lot of papers to finish." She cocked her head and looked at Cara. "Don't you have homework too?"

Cara grinned. "Yes, but that doesn't mean it's going to get done."

"Don't you ever take anything seriously?" Ali asked.

Cara laughed. "Sure, but not homework."

"I don't know how you get away with it. I have to get good grades, or else. And Mom and Dad check to make sure I've done my homework every night."

"Sounds like child abuse."

Ali turned to face Cara, walking backward down the road. "It's called *discipline*. You should try it sometime." She turned again and fell back into step beside her friend. If only she could just let go like Cara and not worry about so much.

"I've got an idea," Cara said. "You're probably not going to like it though." She paused for dramatic effect. "I think we should go check on the horses."

Ali stumbled. "You're just going to walk up to the door and ask Mrs. Marshall if she's starving her horses?"

"Noooo…" Cara grinned. "We're gonna sneak into the barn after dark and see for ourselves."

Ali felt her stomach do a loop-the-loop. "You can't just sneak onto someone's property in the middle of the night!"

"Why not?" Cara gazed back in the direction of the Marshall home. "What if those horses need help?"

Ali wished she were brave enough to say yes. She *did* want to know what was up. But Cara's plan sounded too risky. "Count me out. I don't think it's a good idea. We'd be in a lot of trouble if we got caught."

"Then let's not get caught." Cara punched Ali playfully in the arm. "You're such a goody-two-shoes."

The comment stung. So what if she tried to follow the rules? Just look where breaking the rules had gotten her brother....

"Hey, don't look at me like that." Cara nudged her. "It's not like I'm going to break into Mrs. Marshall's house and hold her for ransom. I just want to make sure those horses are okay."

Ali knew the look on Cara's face. It was going to be difficult to talk her out of this plan. "My mom won't let me hang out with you if you get into trouble."

"Look, Ali…" Cara kicked a rock and watched it skip down the road. "I see the way you look at those Appaloosas when we drive by. You need to quit trying to pretend you don't care." She took a deep breath. "Listen. I know you're still upset about what happened before…you know, with the accident—"

"Cara," Ali said in a warning tone. "I don't want to talk about it."

"All right, all right." Cara shrugged.

They stopped in Ali's driveway. Out of the corner of her eye, Ali saw the curtain move in her brother's bedroom window. She was surprised that he'd pulled himself away from his computer games long enough to glance outside.

Cara shaded her eyes and stared at the window. "Is it weird to have Danny home after so long, and after so much has happened?" she asked. "I used to have kind of a crush on him, but now he freaks me out. He's so quiet."

Ali wasn't sure how to answer. Danny *had* changed since he'd gone to war. He left home ornery and full of himself, but now he was broken and damaged, and with a white-hot anger that could scorch the Nevada desert.

If only she could have her brother back—the way he'd been before, when they were younger. Though he was seven years older, Danny had been a really cool brother, helping her with stuff and looking out for her.

"No, it's not weird having him home," Ali said. "I'm glad he's not in Afghanistan anymore. But it feels…" she searched for the right words, not wanting to sound disloyal to her brother. "It feels kind of like we're living with a stranger. Almost like he doesn't want anything to do with us."

Ali thought back to the phone call telling them that Danny's vehicle had been hit by a roadside bomb. He'd lost the lower part of his left leg in the explosion. She wanted to throw up just remembering it. Danny spent several months after his surgery at an army base in Germany before being flown back to the U.S. He ended up at a military hospital on the East Coast. Her parents had been thrilled—they had a great program for amputees there.

But her brother had been less than excited. He was a difficult patient—which wasn't very different from how he was behaving now, Ali realized. She couldn't even begin to imagine what it would be like to deal with everything that had happened to him. But did he have to take it out on everybody all the time?

The thought made her feel guilty. If Danny had to put up with a missing limb, then she could put up with him being grouchy.

"What does he do all day?" Cara interrupted Ali's thoughts. "With his leg and all, he can't exactly go back to his old life."

Ali scuffed at the dirt with the toe of her shoe. "It's complicated," she began. "The doctors say he could do just about anything he wants if he would wear his prosthetic and do his therapy. But he just hides in his room most of the day. He plays on his computer a lot. Sometimes I hear him fumbling around the house after everyone else has gone to bed. He refuses to wear his prosthetic, and he doesn't want my parents to install a special elevator-type chair that would help him get up and down the stairs more easily."

"Isn't that kind of…you know, strange…having a prosthetic leg lying around?"

Ali giggled. It felt wrong to laugh about it, but really, what else could she do? Did Cara picture Danny's fake leg lying on the coffee table or propped by the front door?

"What's so funny?"

"I'm sorry." The prosthetic *had* freaked her out the first couple of times she'd seen it. "I wasn't laughing at you," she said. "Yeah, it seems odd. He hardly ever wears it. And it's strange to see Danny with part of his leg missing. But he's still my brother." She dug through her backpack, pulled a red licorice vine out of its package, and offered it to her friend.

Cara shoved the whole thing in her mouth and smiled. The red candy lined her teeth like braces. Ali laughed again and started up the front steps. "I'll text you later!"

※

"Is that you, Ali? Come help me with dinner."

Ali kicked off her shoes and went to the kitchen. She was struck by the dark circles under her mother's eyes. Ali hugged her, holding on for an extra long time.

"Thanks, honey, but a hug won't get you out of peeling potatoes." Her mother smiled, pointing to the pot. "Your dad will be home in an hour. We're having meatloaf, green beans, and mashed potatoes."

7

Danny's favorite. Her mom was attempting to lure him downstairs with his favorite meal.

"First, can you tell your brother we'll be eating around five?" She hefted the pot of red potatoes onto the counter and got the potato peeler out of the drawer for Ali.

Ali ran up the steps two at a time, but slowed to a walk when she hit the hallway. The closer she got to her brother's door, the more she felt like she was entering forbidden territory. Like she was entering the dragon's lair.

She could hear rap music playing inside his room. She lifted her hand to knock, but then hesitated. She never knew which Danny she would get when she interrupted him. Sometimes he peeked out with a smile and it almost felt like old times. But most of the time, he jerked the door open with an irritated what-do-you-want look on his face.

She took a deep breath and banged on the door.

"What do you want?" Danny hollered.

"Mom said dinner will be ready in an hour!"

"What?"

The music got quieter; Danny must have lowered the volume a notch. Ali tried again. "MOM SAID DINNER WILL BE READY IN AN HOUR! IT'S YOUR FAVORITE…MEAT-LOAF!"

"Okay."

Ali stared at the dirt bike poster that still hung on Danny's door. The rap returned to its former volume. She shrugged and walked back down the stairs.

"I told him," she said as she picked up the peeler and grabbed the first potato out of the pot.

❦

An hour later, Ali, her mom, and her dad sat around the dinner table, staring at Danny's empty chair.

"I'll go get him," her father offered.

"It's okay." Ali's mom placed her hand on her husband's arm, keeping him in his seat. "He'll be down when he's ready, John. Let's not force the issue. Remember what the soldiers from the Yellow Ribbon Program said. It might take a while for him to readjust."

Her father pursed his lips the way he usually did when he didn't agree with her mother, but he said no more. They ate in silence for a few moments, the only sound the clink of utensils on plates.

"I haven't seen Mrs. Marshall's Appaloosas for a week now," Ali blurted out. She wondered why that particular piece of information had come to mind. There were a hundred other things she could have said.

Her parents stared at her. Ali pushed her food around on her plate.

"Several of the neighbors are looking into the Marshall problem, dear," her mother said. "If someone can figure out how to get through the red tape a little faster, we might be able to get her some help. But right now, she doesn't want any, so it's difficult to do anything."

"There's no need for you to worry about this, Ali," her father said. "But it's nice to see you express interest in horses again. Are you ready to talk about getting another one anytime soon?"

"No, I was just wondering if you knew anything." She pushed back her chair. "I'll take Danny his dinner."

Ali fixed Danny a plate, slipping an extra corn bread muffin onto the tray. She climbed the stairs slowly, not wanting to tip over the glass of milk. This time, she couldn't hear any music in the hallway.

She balanced the tray on one arm and tapped softly on the door. "I've got your dinner." Her voice bounced along the empty hallway. "Danny?" *Maybe he was asleep?* She knocked again.

"Just leave it!"

Ali flinched. Though she wanted to give the door a good kick, she set his plate on the floor instead. *She'd done him a favor bringing him his dinner. He didn't have to be mean about it.* She snatched the extra muffin off the dinner tray, crammed half of it into her mouth, and stomped to her room.

At 9:00, her mother poked her head through Ali's door. "Good night, honey," she said. "I'm turning in early if you don't need any help with your homework?"

"I'm fine. It's almost done." Ali got up to hug her, then glanced down the hall to her brother's door. An empty plate sat on the floor.

"Don't stay up too late," her mother warned. "You've got school tomorrow."

Ten minutes later, a text came from Cara.

Outside your house. Come with me to check horses.

Ali peered out the window. Cara stepped from the shadows and waved. Shaking her head, Ali quietly made her way downstairs, tiptoeing past her parents' bedroom and out the front door.

"Let's go!" Cara whispered.

"Are you nuts?" No way was she going to get caught up in this bucket of trouble. "You should go home, Cara." She glanced around the darkness, hoping none of the neighbors were out for a late-night walk with their dog.

Cara crossed her arms. "How can you just walk away from those horses?" she demanded. "I *know* you care about what's happening to them." She paused. "Besides, I don't want to go there alone."

An upstairs window slid open and both girls froze.

"What are you girls up to?" Danny's suspicious voice cut through the quiet of the night. "Ali, get back in this house!"

His command echoed in her ears and she felt her hands clench. Who did he think he was, ordering her around like this? Like he suddenly cared about her?

She gave Danny a snappy salute, then grabbed Cara by the arm and ran off into the night.

Two

Ali stood at the edge of the Marshall property, uncertainty rooting her to the spot. She was about to commit a felony. Or was trespassing only a misdemeanor? It didn't matter. Once she crossed onto the Marshall place, she was setting herself up for trouble.

"What now?" Ali jumped when her voice came out ten times louder than intended. The neighbor's dogs barked and both girls dropped to a crouch.

When all grew quiet again, Cara whispered, "I don't know exactly. This sounded a lot easier when we talked about it on the bus today...."

"*What?* I thought you had a plan!"

Cara shrugged.

"I can't be out here very long," Ali said. "What if Danny wakes my mom and dad?"

"Well then, we'd better go ahead and have a look in the barn." Cara pulled a small flashlight from her back pocket. "I'll turn this on once we get inside. It doesn't put out much light, but I don't want anyone to be able to see us from the road. For now, be careful where you step. There's a lot of junk lying around."

Ali crept through the shallow ditch. She snagged her foot on an old board hidden in the weeds and fell to her knees, crying out as her teeth clacked together.

The dogs began barking again and a light came on in a window across the street.

"Run!" Cara hissed.

Ali got to her feet and ran, praying that no more surprises hid in the dark. They slipped inside the barn, and she and Cara flattened themselves against the wall. Ali listened for the sound of someone coming after them, but all she could hear was the pounding of her heart and her gasping breath.

The dogs quieted and Ali could hear the chirp of crickets again. Her breathing slowed and her heartbeat returned to near normal. Then her sense of smell kicked in and she grimaced. The barn stank like it hadn't been cleaned in ages.

"Can you smell that?" she whispered. She was surprised to hear the soft nicker of a horse.

"They're here!" Cara clicked on her flashlight and a small beam of light cut through the darkness. The girls crept forward toward the large box stall.

"Oh my gosh!" Ali stared in horror at the two horses, who were pathetically thin and covered in their own filth. Cara's flashlight revealed empty water tubs standing on their sides. There wasn't a scrap of food in sight.

The black gelding was lying down. Was he was too weak to stand? His markings reminded her so much of her pony, Max....

The white mare took a step toward them and her knees buckled, sending her skittering sideways. She crashed against the side of the stall and leaned there, barely holding herself upright.

The neighbor's dogs began barking again.

Ali stood there, taking it all in, but the terrible sight before her made her want to flee. If things looked this bad in the small beam of light, how much worse would the situation be in the broad light of day?

"What are we going to do?" Cara asked.

Ali looked at the darker Appy, seeing the hurt in his body and the pain in his eyes. For a moment, she was transported back to the day her sweet Max was put down and sadness engulfed her.

Ali took a breath, pushing those feelings aside. She couldn't help Max, but she and Cara had to do something for these horses before it was too late.

"They need food and water." Ali motioned for her friend to shine the flashlight around the inside of the barn. "Let's see what we can find."

"There's got to be a water spigot close by," Cara said just as the beam of light landed on a broken water pipe.

"Bummer."

"Go outside and check for a tap close to the barn," Cara said. "I'll look in here for some hay or grain."

Ali grabbed a bucket and found the tap outside. She filled the pail and returned, letting herself into the horses' stall. The black gelding lifted his head, his dull eyes wary and untrusting. "Easy, big guy." She squatted down beside him, placing the water bucket beneath his muzzle.

The white mare nickered and took a feeble step forward, begging for a drink. "It's your turn next," Ali assured her. "I think your stablemate is a little worse off than you."

The gelding stuck his muzzle into the bucket and sloshed the water around with his lips, but he didn't drink at first. Then he seemed to come out of his stupor and greedily gulped the cool water.

"Maybe you'd better not let him have too much at one time," Cara said from the hayloft. "Looks like they haven't had anything to drink for a while. Too much now might make them sick."

Just then the gelding choked, coughing hard and tipping over the bucket.

"Oh, no!" Ali jumped to her feet. What had she done?

"What happened?" Cara climbed out of the hayloft. "Is he okay?"

Ali looked from Cara to the coughing Appy, unsure what to do. She'd never seen a horse choke before. The Heimlich maneuver was definitely out of the question.

The gelding coughed and wheezed, then collapsed onto his side, his legs thrashing against the filthy floor of the stall. After a few more seconds, he rolled into a more upright position. The coughing had stopped, but his breathing was still heavy. Ali wasn't sure if this was a good sign or not.

The mare stumbled over, pushing the bucket aside as she tried to suck up the spilled water that pooled in a muddy mess on the floor.

"Ugh! That is so gross. Don't drink that." Ali gently pushed the mare away, then picked up the bucket and went to fetch more water.

When she returned, Ali tried to make sure the mare sipped the liquid slowly. It was almost impossible. She buried her muzzle in the bucket, and Ali had to keep pulling it back after every few sips. Cara tried to help, gently tugging on the mare's head. It was a difficult task, even with two of them.

When they finished, Ali offered water to the gelding again. He hesitated, but finally drank.

"That has to be a good sign," Cara said. "If he refused water, he might be too far gone."

"Did you find any food?"

Cara shook her head. "Not a single stem of hay or a handful of oats to be found. We could pick some of the grass from next door. It doesn't look like they've mowed their lawn in a while."

They moved silently to the neighbor's yard and picked as much of the new summer grass as they could carry. When they reentered the barn, the white mare whinnied weakly and pawed at the wall. The crickets grew quiet at the sudden banging on the wooden wall, but at least the neighbor dogs didn't bark this time.

"*Shhhh.*" Cara placed her hand on the mare's nose, trying to quiet her. The horse smelled the grass and stretched her lips toward the bunch Cara held in her other hand. "Wow, she's really hungry!"

"I'm going to try feeding the black horse." Ali hunkered down and placed the fresh blades of grass right under his nose, but he barely looked at her. She tickled the underside of his chin with the blades. "He doesn't seem to want any."

"That's not good." Cara paused for a moment and the white mare whinnied loudly, demanding more food.

The neighbor's dogs began barking again. "Keep her quiet or we're gonna get caught!" Ali groaned. "Better turn off the flashlight so nobody sees it if they look outside." With the click of the switch, the barn was plunged into total darkness.

A moment later, a bright beam of light cut through the barn, startling Ali and blinding her with its brightness.

"What's going on out here?"

"Oh, no!" Cara hissed, opening the door to the stall. "It's Mrs. Marshall! Run!"

Three

Ali scrambled to her feet and bolted out the stall door behind Cara. They tore through the barn, the light from Mrs. Marshall's flashlight bouncing crazily around the room.

"Stop!" the old lady hollered. "You kids get back here! I'm going to call the police!"

They ran out the back door of the barn and pounded down the road. Ali pumped her arms, trying to gain more speed. She didn't know where they were going, and she didn't really care. She'd been a fool to go to Mrs. Marshall's place. Her parents were going to be furious.

After what seemed like forever, they stopped in the cover of a large tree. Ali bent over and sucked in huge gulps of air. She'd never run so fast or so far in her entire life. When her vision cleared, she looked around and noticed they were in sight of her house.

"You okay?" Cara panted.

Ali took several more deep breaths, trying to calm down before answering. "No, I'm *not* okay! We're going to get in a lot of trouble!"

She stared at her house, looking for a sign that her parents had noticed she was gone. It was dark and quiet. Did she dare hope that Danny had kept this adventure to himself?

"We're going to be fine," Cara assured her. "We got away. No one followed us."

Ali took a good hard look at her friend. "Just because we got away with it doesn't make it right. We shouldn't have gone onto Mrs. Marshall's property. She saw us. She could have us arrested."

"Maybe we will get into trouble, but at least now we know what happened to the horses. They need help. What are we going to do?"

Ali tried to come up with an answer. She couldn't get the image of the gelding, his ribs sticking out, and the poor mare, who could hardly hold her own weight, out of her mind. "I don't think the black one will make it much longer," she admitted.

Cara jammed her hands into her pockets and stared up at the moon. "We're going to have to turn in Mrs. Marshall. Maybe Animal Control will do something this time, once they know things are even worse than before."

"But if we report her, we'll have to admit we were in her barn," Ali said. "We could get in lots of trouble."

"Maybe we don't give our names?"

Ali thought for a moment. "With Caller ID, they'd know exactly where the call came from," she said. "We wouldn't remain anonymous for very long." She crossed her arms and paced a few steps up and back. How had she gotten involved with this?

Ali took a deep breath and slowly let it out. She'd gotten involved because two horses were in desperate need of attention. The adults were taking too long. "We'll figure things out in the morning," she said. "It's too late to call anyone at this hour. We gave them water and some grass. Hopefully, that will be enough to get them through the next few hours. Right now I've got to get back into the house before my parents find out I'm gone. I'll see you tomorrow."

She ran up the front walk, slowing when she reached the creaky porch steps. The door was unlocked, just as she'd left it. She held her breath as she entered the house and crept past her parents' bedroom. She felt lower than a snake's belly in a tire rut.

A muffled cry came from Danny's room. She paused at the top of the stairs, listening. It came again, like something from a spooky movie, and the hair on her arms stood straight up. She crept closer and pressed her ear against the wood. Danny was moaning and thrashing, the bedsprings squealing in protest.

"Danny?" She spoke softly, trying not to wake their parents. He was probably having another bad dream—he'd had a lot of them since he'd returned. They made her mom really upset.

"Danny?" She turned the doorknob, finding it unlocked. Her brother let out another tortured howl.

Ali stepped into the room, not sure what to do. "Danny!" she hissed. How could their parents sleep through all this noise? "Danny, wake up!" She took him by the shoulder, shaking him gently.

Danny sat up bolt upright and lashed out. His knuckles grazed Ali's cheek and she fell backwards, her feet tangled in the twisted covers.

"Ali...?" Danny sounded confused—but also more like his old self. He leaned over the side of the bed and peered at her. "What happened?"

"You were having a bad dream. I tried to wake you, but…" She rubbed her cheek as she stood. Had he left a mark?

A flash of regret passed over Danny's face, then his eyes narrowed and his mouth hardened into a thin line. He pointed toward the door. "I told everyone to stay out of my room. You shouldn't have come in here. Now get out!"

"What's going on up there?" Their father's voice rose from the bottom of the staircase.

Ali's mouth went dry. Would Danny be angry enough to tell her parents that she'd snuck out of the house? She locked eyes with her brother, willing him not to say anything.

"Everything's fine, Dad," Danny hollered. "I'll see you in the morning." He waited until he heard the downstairs bedroom door close, then turned to Ali. "Don't say anything to Mom and Dad about this, okay? They worry about me enough already—especially Mom." He tucked his injured leg back under the sheets, then rolled over and pulled the covers up around him, effectively dismissing her.

Ali rubbed her cheek. She'd only been trying to help. Danny hadn't meant to hit her, but the meanness in his voice afterward had been deliberate.

Danny insisted he was fine. But the truth was, he wasn't. He needed help. Why couldn't he see that? Why couldn't her parents do something?

Back in her room, Ali stepped out of her jeans and into her pajamas. Morning would be here soon and she'd have to figure out what to do about the Appaloosas. And her parents would have to decide what to do about Danny.

"Well, what's the verdict?" Cara asked the next morning as soon as Ali sat down on the bus. "If we don't do something quickly, those horses won't make it."

As the bus passed the Marshall place, both girls turned to scrutinize the property. There was no sign of the horses or Mrs. Marshall. She hoped the poor animals could hold on a bit longer. Ali wrestled with her thoughts a moment, then turned to Cara. "We've got to do it. We have to make sure Animal Control knows how bad things have gotten. There's no way they can let Mrs. Marshall off with just a lecture again if they see the state of those horses. This time, they'll *have* to do something."

Cara nodded solemnly and they rode the rest of the way in silence.

The morning classes dragged, but lunch finally arrived. The girls ate quickly, then left the cafeteria to use the phone outside the nurse's station.

Cara looked the number up on her cell phone and Ali did the dialing. Her hands shook and she tried to hand the phone to Cara, but her friend refused to take it.

Just as Ali was ready to hang up, someone answered. "Animal Control. How may I direct your call?"

This is it, Ali thought. It was time for her to step up and be brave. She opened her mouth to speak, but no words came out.

"Hello? Are you there?"

Ali thought of the horses, desperate for water and food, and found her courage *and* her voice. She took a deep breath. "Er, hi…. I can't give you my name, but I want to report a case of animal abuse."

Four

Ali spent the rest of the school day worrying. Had they made the call in time? Would the horses be okay? She kept expecting the door to the classroom to fly open to reveal a uniformed officer, who would escort her and Cara off to juvenile hall.

"There's no way they can trace that call to us," Cara told her as they boarded the school bus. She plopped into the seat by the window in the first empty row. "Anyway, we did the right thing."

"That's true, but my parents will still hit the roof if they find out we snuck out and went to Mrs. Marshall's." Ali took a deep breath and let it out slowly. "But I'll take a punishment if it means we saved those horses' lives."

The bus driver closed the door with a noisy bang and pulled out onto the road.

"Guess Jamie got a ride home from school," Cara said. "Hey, look what I found online this morning." She held her cell phone up for Ali to see. "There's a great photo of him in the newspaper. He helped restore a bunch of bikes so they could give them to foster kids who didn't have any."

Ali stared at the photo of the tall, dark-haired boy with the nice smile. He seemed like a pretty great guy. She raised an eyebrow at Cara. "Stalk people much?" They both burst out laughing.

"Seriously though," Cara said. "I think he's cute. He smiled at you yesterday. I thought you might want to know a little more about him."

"If I wanted to know more, I would have looked him up myself." Ali *had* thought about it, actually, but she wouldn't tell Cara that.

Cara elbowed Ali and pointed out the window. At first all Ali could see were some white trucks parked alongside the road. One of them was hitched to a horse trailer. As the bus drew closer, she realized that the vehicles were from Animal Control. And they were outside Mrs. Marshall's house.

They had come! Their phone call had worked! She wanted to pump her fist in the air and yell, "YES!" But that would give them away.

Ali and Cara quietly slapped a high five. "Let's get off at this stop so we can see what's happening," Cara suggested.

Ali shook her head. "I don't think we should."

As soon as the bus stopped, Cara was out of her seat and heading toward the door. Ali had no choice but to follow. But when Cara started walking straight toward the Marshall place, Ali balked. "What are you doing?"

"Come on!" Cara waved her forward. "Don't you want to see what's happening up close?"

"I don't think we should go near that house. Mrs. Marshall might recognize us. Let's take the long way around."

"But I want to see the horses," Cara said. "I want make sure they're okay. Come on." She linked her arm through Ali's, dragging her forward.

Ali decided it would be best to just go along. She didn't want to draw attention by putting up a fight.

Several neighbors were gathered along the roadside, watching the Animal Control officers. "Finally!" one woman said. "Somebody finally got through to them."

"It took Animal Control long enough," another replied. "Now maybe we'll be able to get some help for those poor horses, even if Mrs. Marshall is still being stubborn."

Ali stood on her toes, trying to catch a glimpse of the horses. The black Appy was on his feet, tied to a fence post. Her heart broke for him. His head hung down and his legs wobbled like he was ready to collapse.

It had all been worth it. Ali and Cara had almost gotten caught, but the horses had been rescued.

A part of her felt sorry for Mrs. Marshall. Surely she hadn't meant to starve her horses. She had always taken good care of them before this. Maybe the rumors were true—maybe she was going senile. Nobody in her right mind would treat an animal this way.

They were just past the small crowd when Cara stopped. "Look! That's Jamie holding the white Appy. What's he doing here?" She waved and Jamie's brows drew together like he was trying to figure out who she was.

Dread washed over Ali. "His dad is probably the vet on this project. Keep walking," she said, but she couldn't help glancing back. Mrs. Marshall was standing right there, wringing her hands.

Jamie was comforting the Appaloosa mare while his dad examined her. The poor horse was so filthy that it was hard to tell the difference between her leopard spots and the dirt on her coat. Jamie looked up again and this time he seemed to recognize Ali and Cara. He nodded, but the smile was missing from his face. She could tell that he was upset about the horses.

Ali nodded back to him and kept walking. They made it another five steps before a sharp voice rang out.

"Hey, you girls over there! Stop!" Mrs. Marshall hollered. "I think that's them," she said to the Animal Control officer. "Those are the girls who were in my barn last night. This is all their fault!"

Cara dragged Ali straight down the road. "Don't stop," she muttered. "Don't look back. Don't even acknowledge that you heard her. Just keep walking. With any luck, they'll say Mrs. Marshall is crazy."

Ali moved as fast as she could without making it look like she was running away. She glanced over her shoulder and saw the officers staring, but nobody tried to stop them.

Ali and Cara walked around the corner, then broke into a run. Only after they were several streets away did they slow down.

"Do you think they'll come after us?" Ali shifted her backpack farther up on her shoulder while she tried to regain her breath.

Cara looked behind them. "I don't think so. They would have stopped us by now. Besides, who's going to believe a nutty old lady who starves her horses?"

They walked the next block in silence, each lost in her thoughts. "We should check with Animal Control later and see how the horses are doing," Ali said.

"Or we could wait and ask Jamie on the bus tomorrow."

"You're incorrigible!" Ali waved goodbye and walked up her front steps. She pushed the door open, dropped her backpack in the hallway, and cut through the living room on her way to the kitchen for a snack. She stopped and stared.

Danny was sitting on the couch, watching TV. She wasn't used to seeing him out of his room.

"What are you looking at?" He picked up the remote control and switched to the sports channel.

"Er…nothing…," Ali sputtered.

Her mother had left a note on the kitchen counter saying she was getting her hair cut. Ali spied a pan of freshly baked brownies. She cut Danny an extra big piece and a smaller one for herself, then poured two glasses of milk.

She balanced the plates on her arm, grabbed the drinks, and walked to the living room. Her hands shook as she set everything down on the coffee table.

She took a seat on the end of the couch—not too close because Danny got restless if he felt boxed in. He gave her the stink eye, but then mumbled a barely audible "thanks" as he took a brownie. Ali smiled. It wasn't much, but it felt like a beginning.

She reached for her own brownie and settled back on the couch, telling herself not to get too excited. Danny had only been home for a month. With everything that had happened, it might take a while to get back into the brother-sister thing again.

Ali picked at her brownie, eating one small piece at a time. She had to make it last so she could sit here until she worked up the nerve to start a conversation. Danny wasn't much for talking these days—unless it was to one of his military friends still in Afghanistan, or someone he played video games with.

"It's a nice day outside," she said. "Do you want me to open the curtains?"

Danny took another huge bite and shook his head. "Nope. I like it just fine the way it is." He turned up the volume on the TV.

O-kaaaay.... Her heart sank a little. *Nothing like talking to a brick wall.* Her appetite vanished and she set the remainder of her snack on the coffee table.

Danny must have sensed he'd upset her. "It's all good, sis," he said with an attempt at a smile. "I'm only going to be down here until the mailman comes. I'm waiting for some computer stuff to be delivered."

"Is it something cool?"

Danny shrugged. "I ordered a new video card. The games changed a lot in the time I was gone, and I'm trying to play catch up with the rest of my online group. This card should do the trick."

Ali smiled and nodded. Danny lived inside of his computer these days, hiding away from the world.

The doorbell rang and Danny sprang up without reaching for his crutches first. Ali watched in horror as her brother attempted the first step on a leg that wasn't there. He went down hard, landing with a grunt.

"Danny!" She ran to help, but the look in his eyes warned her she'd better not touch him.

Danny let out a string of not-so-pretty words as he rolled onto his side and held his wounded leg. "Get the door!" he commanded. "Make sure the postman leaves that video card."

Video card? Danny had fallen, but the only thing that mattered to him was a stupid computer card? There was a whole lot more going on here than she knew about, and it was beginning to frighten her.

Five

If the postman heard the commotion, he didn't let on. He'd left the package on the steps, and when Ali opened the door he was smiling and waving as he drove off.

Danny was still on the floor when Ali reentered the house, but now he was sitting upright with his back against the coffee table.

"What happened?" she asked.

"Nothing." Danny scooted over to the couch and used it to pull himself up to his feet. He reached for his crutch.

"You're hurt." Ali wanted to go to his side, but she didn't dare. He didn't want help. Kind of like Mrs. Marshall, now that she thought about it. What was it with people, anyway?

"It's not a big deal," he muttered. "Sometimes I just forget..."

"Forget what?" She sucked in a quick breath. "You forgot...that you're missing your leg?" *How could he forget something like that?*

"Quit looking like a hurt puppy, and *don't you dare* cry." Danny picked up his dirty dishes and made his way slowly to the kitchen. He turned back when he reached the doorway. "And don't say anything to Mom and Dad about this, you hear?" His voice softened a bit. "They worry enough about me as it is."

Ali wanted to scream at him, *It's their job to worry about you! They're your parents!* But she didn't.

"Ali?" Danny gave her a hard look. "I mean it. Don't say a word."

This was something her parents *should* know about. Why did her brother get to make all the rules?

Ali placed her hands on her hips and stood up a little straighter. "I won't tell Mom and Dad about this if you don't tell them about me leaving the house last night." She held her breath, hoping her false bravado would work.

"And what exactly was it you were doing?"

Ali tried to stand even taller, but she had reached the top of her five-foot, zero inches height. "Nothing," she said, using her own brother's word as she tried to keep her voice from shaking.

A hint of a smile touched Danny's lips. "Deal," he said, and hobbled into the kitchen.

She let out the breath she'd been holding and mentally patted herself on the back. This was the first time she'd ever stood up to Danny. It hadn't been as hard as she'd thought it would be.

She put a little swagger in her step as she climbed the stairs to her room, but she promised herself: no more crazy adventures.

≋

Ali was almost done with her English paper when she heard her father's heavy footsteps on the stairs. He rarely ever came upstairs. Was he coming to visit her or Danny? She laid her

29

laptop on the bed and sat up a little straighter, tuning into the sounds in the hall. The footfalls passed her bedroom and a second later, she heard a loud rap on Danny's door.

"Danny?"

After a slight delay, her brother responded. "Yes, sir?"

"Dinner will be ready in five minutes," her dad said. "I expect you to be at the table tonight."

"I'm not hungry. I'll eat later."

Ali got off her bed and tiptoed to the door, placing her ear against the wood.

"That wasn't a request," her dad said. "It's an order. We'll see you at the table in five minutes."

An order? It sounded like her dad and brother were in a showdown. Who would win? Ali's bet was on Danny.

The footsteps came her way and she scrambled back to the bed. She'd barely gotten herself settled when her father knocked lightly, then opened her door. Ali tried to look nonchalant, but she could tell her dad knew she'd been listening.

"I'm sure you heard," he said. "Dinner is in five minutes."

Ali turned off her laptop. This was getting interesting. On her way down the stairs, she remembered her deal with Danny: neither of them would tell their parents about last night. Her insides went a little wonky. She hoped he would keep his side of the bargain.

She took her seat at the dinner table. Danny appeared a minute later. She wondered how he must feel to be grown up enough to go fight a war, yet be ordered to the dinner table like a little kid.

Her mother said a quick blessing and everyone dug in. Ali took a couple of pieces of chicken and some brussels sprouts—

green balls of death, Danny called them—and filled the rest of her plate with mashed potatoes.

"So, we just hired some new workers that I'm expected to train," her father began. He loaded his plate with several pieces of chicken and some potatoes, skipping the brussels sprouts. "I just hope I'm not training my replacement."

Ali's mom handed her the butter. "I'm sure you aren't, John. They wouldn't know what to do without you."

Their dad turned to Danny. "How was your day?"

"Fine," Danny grunted through a mouthful of chicken.

Her mother changed the subject. "I hear Animal Control took those poor horses away from old Mrs. Marshall today."

Ali tried hard not to choke. She looked at Danny, but he just shrugged. He had no way of knowing where she'd gone anyway.

"I heard too. And Russell said the horses are in pretty bad shape," her father continued.

Ali pushed the brussels sprouts around on her plate. She'd forgotten her father's friend worked for Animal Control. Her appetite was suddenly gone.

"Apparently Mrs. Marshall says two girls broke into her barn last night," her father said. "And she saw them again today in the crowd at her house."

Uh-oh. Ali swallowed hard. A piece of chicken lodged in her throat and refused to go down.

"Do you think it was somebody you know, Allison?"

He had used her given name—did he suspect her? If Russell was there today, then he probably saw her and Cara. *So much for the idea that no one would believe Mrs. Marshall.*

Her family's eyes were all on her. Ali thought about lying. Surely they'd believe her over Mrs. Marshall? She fidgeted with the silverware while trying to make up her mind. If she told the truth, she was in a lot of trouble. But could she lie to her parents?

Ali looked her father straight in the eye. "Last night Cara and I snuck out to check on the horses. We just wanted to see if they were okay. They looked really horrible the last time we saw them." She dropped her eyes to her plate and waited for her punishment.

"And was it also you who called Animal Control?" her mother asked.

Ali nodded.

Her father drummed his fingers on the table. "Well, I'm a little befuddled about what to do here," he said as he glanced at his wife. "On one hand, you knowingly went against our rules by sneaking out of the house. You put yourself in potential danger." He paused a moment and gave her the Dad stare. "On the other hand, you girls most likely saved the lives of those two horses. And it's good to see you showing some interest in horses again."

Ali felt a surge of hope. She couldn't exactly agree that she was getting back into horses again, but saving those horses had to count for something, didn't it? "Dad, you should have seen them," she said. "They were so skinny and dirty…"

Ali's mom looked concerned. "Why didn't you come to us about this, instead of sneaking out in the middle of the night?" she asked. "We might have been able to help."

Ali didn't want to admit that it had been a foolish impulse to run off with Cara. Or that she'd done it partially to get even with her brother. "You and Dad were already in bed when Cara came by," she explained. "Besides, you guys have enough to worry about with Danny. You don't need to worry about somebody else's horses too."

She felt the weight of her brother's stare and instantly wished that she'd left that last part off. She folded her hands in her lap and kept her eyes on her half-eaten dinner.

Her mother shifted uncomfortably in her chair. "Ali, your father and I always have time for your concerns. I hope that next time you'll come to us instead of making an unwise choice."

Ali wanted to crawl under the table. She'd managed—with only a couple of short sentences—to upset everyone.

Her father cleared his throat. "Your mother and I will take a little time to think about the appropriate punishment," he said. "I'm proud that you had the good judgment to admit the truth to us and the courage to stand up for those defenseless animals in the first place. But sneaking out of the house at night is very dangerous. Who knows what could have happened to you?"

"I'm disappointed with you, Allison," her mother said. "Running around in the dark and trespassing on other people's property—even though some good might have come out of it this time. Really, what were you thinking, dear?"

Ali hung her head and mumbled. "I guess I wasn't really thinking. I'm sorry."

"For starters…" Her dad pinned her with another hard stare. "You won't be allowed to see Cara for the next week."

"Yes, sir," she said. Tomorrow was Saturday; Cara's parents were planning to take them into town. She hoped she hadn't just gotten Cara into trouble, too. She would have to call and let Cara know what had happened. That is, if her parents didn't take away her phone and computer privileges too.

Her dad turned his attention to Danny. "And, while I'm at it," he began. "We're going to have a few more changes around here…."

33

Danny put down his fork and sat up straighter in his chair.

"Son, we know you're struggling right now; your injury is just one of the many things you've got to deal with," their father said. "But you can't stay holed up in your room all day doing nothing but playing on that computer. I know you don't want to talk to us or a therapist just yet, but you do have to get back to a regular routine. No more putting it off."

Their mom took her son's hand. "Sometime in the near future, you might even want to think about getting a part-time job or furthering your education. We'll help any way we can."

Ali saw Danny's jaw tighten and he quietly slipped his hand out of their mother's grasp. It was obvious he wasn't pleased about getting these ultimatums. She glanced nervously toward her parents. How far could they push her brother before he blew up and went back to his room?

"Maybe we should see about setting up another appointment with the Veteran's Administration?" her father continued. "You missed the last one. They've called several times to try to reschedule. They're a good resource, son." He paused for a moment. "I know you're a grown man, Danny, and you've been off to fight a war, and have seen things we can't imagine. But moping around the house doing nothing isn't helping you move forward."

"*Yes, sir,*" Danny said sharply, and pushed back from the table. He grabbed his crutches and limped out of the room.

"We just want what's best for you," their mom said as she followed her son's progress with sad eyes. She turned to her husband. "I don't think that went over very well, John. What are we going to do?"

Ali felt like a fly on the wall. It was as if her parents had forgotten she was there, as though they'd forgotten they were mad at her.

She knew she shouldn't be jealous of her brother, but in a weird way, she did envy how much of their attention he had. She needed her parents too. Her life hadn't stopped just because Danny came home.

Her father looked old and tired. "I'm not sure how to reach him," he admitted. "Outside of hog-tying him, tossing him in the back of the truck, and driving him down to the VA, I can't force him to get help."

"Help for what, exactly?" Ali asked.

Ali saw the unasked question pass from her mother to her father: *Should we tell her?*

Her father shook his head. "Allison, would you please clean off the table and leave your mother and me to talk?"

It was an order, not a question, so Ali did what she was told, but she felt angry. Why did they always keep her in the dark about this stuff? She lived here too. Didn't she have a right to know what was going on with her own brother?

Standing in the kitchen, she listened to her parents speak in hushed tones and tried to decipher what they were saying. She turned on the dishwasher, then tiptoed over to the doorway to listen. Several words jumped out at her: *Veteran's Affairs, psychologist, Wounded Warrior Project, Disabled Vets, PTSD.*

This sounded important. Her parents probably thought they were shielding her from things she was too young to comprehend. But they were wrong.

Ali returned to her room and switched on her computer. Maybe she could help. She *wanted* to help her brother. And right now, that meant doing some research, starting with discovering what *PTSD* meant.

Six

PTSD: *Post-traumatic Stress Disorder.* Ali clicked the icon to print the eight-page booklet from the website for the National Center for PTSD. She read over the information and was shocked to see how many of the symptoms Danny had.

Agitated and jumpy. *Yup.*

Feelings of being tired, empty, and numb. *You betcha.*

Desire to be alone all the time. *Sooo true!*

Less patience than normal. *You got that right.*

Avoids certain people or situations. *Right on.*

Lashes out and overreacts to small misunderstandings. *Bingo!*

Ali sighed. She wasn't a doctor or a psychologist, but she was pretty sure that Danny had PTSD. She wondered: Did *he* know?

She read that PTSD was common in those with combat experience. That wasn't a surprise. Another website said that 41 percent of the soldiers coming back from the wars in Iraq and Afghanistan had it.

Ali thought about the thousands of other families out there dealing with this problem just like her family was. The thought made her sad.

She was relieved to read that people with PTSD could return to their normal lives. She doubted she could get her brother back to the way he was when they were kids, but maybe there was hope he could at least get past the troubles he was having now.

Ali picked up her phone to call Cara. She wasn't sure if she wanted to share her concerns about Danny, but she definitely needed to tell her she'd been grounded.

"Of all the rotten luck," Cara said. "Your dad just happens to have a friend there when Mrs. Marshall points her finger at us, and now we can't hang out for the next week? Bummer. We were supposed to go to the movies tomorrow."

"I know."

"The movie we were going to see will be showing for a couple weeks though, so I'll wait until you can go with me," Cara offered.

"Really?" Ali said. "That would be awesome!"

"It wouldn't be as much fun watching it with my little sister," Cara said. "It really stinks that you're grounded. And your parents probably think I'm a bad influence now."

Ali laughed. "Well, you kind of are." But in the back of her mind, she heard one of her dad's tough questions: *Did someone twist your arm and force you into making that bad decision?*

"I guess it *was* my idea," Cara admitted. "Hey, do you think your parents will tell mine?"

"I don't know. They didn't mention it. I'm sorry, I just had to tell the truth. They asked me point-blank."

"Oh, that's okay. You were brave to admit it."

Cara thought that she *was brave?* "Nah," Ali said. "I'm not brave. I was just more afraid of what my parents would do if they caught me lying. I still don't know what my main punishment is going to be. Being grounded from hanging out with you was just part of it."

"Ugh," Cara commiserated. "Well, I'd better get going. I've got to get up early tomorrow for the horseshoer."

"Okay."

"Ali. You know we've got two horses. You can ride my mom's anytime you feel like it. You should really think about it."

Ali cringed. Why wouldn't people stop trying to get her back into horses? "Look, I just don't feel like riding anymore, okay?"

There was a long pause, and then Cara spoke up, her voice much harsher than Ali had ever heard it. "Look, *Allison*." Cara put heavy emphasis on her name. "You and I *both* know that you love horses. I see how sad you look when you see me riding Dumpling, and I saw the way you looked at those Appaloosas *every* time we went by the Marshall place. And you helped rescue them! It's bad enough that you lie to me and tell me you don't want to ride anymore. But you're lying to yourself too."

Two different people had used her you're-in-trouble name today. It was bad enough when her parents did it. But now her best friend—the one who got her into trouble in the first place—was getting in on the act!

She thought about hanging up, but that wouldn't be fair.

Cara really loved horses. And she cared about Ali. She was only trying to get her interested again in something she used to love.

Ali let out the angry breath she'd been holding. It wasn't fair for her to take things out on her friend just because she was upset about getting grounded. Cara *had* asked her to sneak out, but *Ali* had chosen to accept the invitation. She only had herself to blame.

She took a deep breath. "Look, I don't mean to be a jerk about this. I *do* care about the horses we rescued. I want to see them get better. But after Max, and all the stuff that went on with my brother afterward…I just don't feel like riding yet, or doing anything with horses. Okay?"

"Wait, is that why Danny enlisted?" Cara sounded confused. "Because of your accident?"

"Cara. I don't want to talk about it anymore." If she hadn't tried to follow Danny, Max wouldn't have broken his leg, she wouldn't have broken her arm, Danny wouldn't have joined the military, and everything would be different.

How had things gotten so messed up?

"I need to go," Ali said. "I don't feel so good." She hung up the phone and lay down on the bed. She felt hollow inside. Cara had touched on a raw spot that Ali had never really discussed with anyone—not even Cara. She drew the covers up to her chin and wiped a tear that slid down her cheek. *If only I'd left Max in the barn and stayed home that day… things might have turned out differently.*

❧

Ali woke the next morning to the sound of a truck and trailer bumping up her driveway. She sat up and rubbed her eyes. They felt puffy from crying the night before.

She rolled from her bed, pulled on her jeans and T-shirt, and made her way down the stairs. Grabbing her shoes from the hallway, Ali scooted out the back door, curious to see what the commotion was about. It was Saturday morning—not much happened around her house on the weekends.

Her parents stood by the barn. "Just back it into the corral area," her dad told the driver.

Ali watched the man get back into the truck and maneuver it into position. What was in the trailer? The truck hit a bump and Ali heard a wary snort. It sounded suspiciously like a horse.

The driver turned off the engine and got out. He wore a baseball cap; a pair of sunglasses shielded his eyes from the bright Nevada sun. The man looked vaguely familiar, but with the hat and glasses, she couldn't figure out why. Then Jamie Forrester got out of the passenger side.

Her heart took a little jump. What was *he* doing here?

And then it dawned on her: Jamie had been with the rescued Appaloosas yesterday. Jamie, plus horse trailer, plus snorting horse in the trailer equaled...

"Let's get them unloaded," the older man said. He handed a lead rope to Jamie.

They opened the trailer door and the man in the hat unloaded a white horse with leopard spots. Ali almost didn't recognize her. Mrs. Marshall's mare was clean now, but the protruding ribs and painful thinness gave her away.

Slow, faltering hoofbeats echoed on the trailer floor. Jamie led the black Appaloosa out of the trailer. The gelding had also been cleaned up, but the signs of abuse were fully evident.

Even though they had been bathed and brushed, the sight of the pathetic animals made Ali cringe. How could anyone let this happen? Even if Mrs. Marshall was senile, wasn't there some part of her that knew something needed to be done to keep these animals healthy? She stared at the horses. Both had prominent backbones, with bony and frail withers and shoulders. Their heads appeared bigger than normal because their bodies were so thin.

Why are these horses at our house? She glanced at her parents, looking for a clue, but they were busy talking with the older man.

The horses shuffled carefully into the pen, as if they only had enough energy to go so far. Jamie removed their halters and waved Ali over.

Her stomach began a slow roll as all the evidence added up. She shook her head and backed up a step.

Jamie waved to her again, but Ali stood where she was, her feet rooted to the ground. There were horses in her backyard and her parents just stood there, as if this sort of thing happened every day. They beamed at her liked they'd just done something pretty amazing. And it might have been pretty awesome—*if* she wanted another horse. But Ali didn't. Especially when one of them reminded her so much of Max.

Seven

Seriously, what were her parents thinking? Ali thought about turning and running away, maybe hiding someplace, but she didn't want to act like a baby in front of everyone. Jamie motioned again, and then her parents called her over to the corrals. Ali was dumbfounded. How could they possibly think this was a good idea?

Reluctantly she walked over, hands in pockets, hoping she didn't stumble and fall flat on her face in front of the small gathering.

The closer she got to the pen, the more her eyes were drawn to the black horse. Her heart pounded in her chest. Were these horses going to be staying here for a few days? *Or longer?*

The gelding took a step and stumbled, almost pitching headfirst into the fence.

Her mom quickly moved toward the horse, a concerned look on her face. She reached through the fence and put a comforting hand on his neck.

Ali could feel the weight of everyone's stares as they watched her walk toward the corrals. Just thirty more steps and she'd be there. Her shoes felt like they had twenty pounds of lead in them. The closer she got to the horses, the harder it was to take the next step.

The driver came forward. "Hi, Ali, I'm Jim Forrester. I haven't seen you since the accident with your pony." He extended his hand.

Dr. Forrester? Jamie's dad? The veterinarian who had tried to help Max but ended up having to put him to sleep? No wonder he looked so familiar. She stared at the vet's extended hand until her dad cleared his throat loudly. She reached out and pumped the doctor's hand. She shouldn't feel badly toward him. The vet had done everything he could to help Max.

"I want to thank you for saving these horses' lives," Dr. Forrester said. "Another few days and they might not have made it."

Ali's father spoke up. "The way the girls went about it wasn't the best, but we're proud of Ali for being part of the rescue. These horses deserve better." He smiled at Ali. "That's why we decided to bring them here."

"Look, Ali," her mother said. "I know you might be shocked. I guess we probably should have told you we were doing this. But your dad's friend from Animal Control called us late last night and told us about the stabling difficulties they were having. The horses needed a place to get healthy again. You cared enough to see that these horses were rescued. You're the perfect person to care for them now."

Ali didn't know what to say. She watched as the white mare lowered her head to the ground, hungrily lipping a small weed that grew in the sand. The horses were malnourished and scrawny. What if she couldn't care for them properly? What if she tried and the horses died anyway?

Dr. Forrester must have seen the panic on her face. "You won't be alone in this, Ali," he reassured her. "Your parents

43

will help any way they can, and Jamie and I will be with you every step of the way. We've worked on several of these cases."

Ali glanced in the boy's direction. He smiled at her and she wondered if he remembered her trampling on his toes that day on the bus. He gave her a quick wink, like they shared a secret, and Ali decided that he did. She could feel her cheeks getting hot.

"It's going to take a group effort," Dr. Forrester said. "We'll be over here every day for the first week, so we can be sure things are going okay." He grabbed his clipboard from the front seat of the truck. "We usually don't put distressed horses into a home quite this quickly, but the only large animal pen they have at Animal Control is filled with some llamas they rescued last week. Your parents assured me you're really good with horses. And I remember you took great care of your pony, so I'm sure these animals will be on the path to better health soon."

Dr. Forrester leaned on the fence, looking at the Appys. "Jamie can tell you a couple of things while I fill out the paperwork and go over the horse care plan with your folks. Then I'll be over to explain it to you in detail."

Ali watched the adults walk up to the house. A movement in Danny's window drew her attention. Ali looked up in time to see the curtain drop back into place. Danny was spying on them—again. What did he think about the new additions to their household? She shrugged. Danny didn't even want to come downstairs. He probably didn't care about anything outside.

"Ali?" Jamie hesitated. "Didn't you know the horses were coming to your house?"

Ali shoved her hands into her pockets and shook her head.

He moved closer—too close for comfort, so she backed up

a step. He smelled good, like horses and a warm summer day. She took one more step back for good measure.

"Are you okay with this?" She could hear the doubt in his voice. "These horses are in a world of hurt, Ali. They're going to demand a whole lot of care. Your parents told us what a good horsewoman you are, but these horses are really in bad shape. They're going to demand a lot more work than what you were used to with your healthy pony."

Ali let her eyes wander to the Appaloosas. "What happens if I don't want to do it?" she asked. "What if I say no?"

"Then we'd have to find somebody else who can do it on short notice." Jamie frowned. "We've got no place to put them right now, except maybe in the horse trailer, and that wouldn't be very good. My dad says horses that are this far down have an impaired immune system. They're really susceptible to getting sick. Living in a trailer would make the risk even worse."

Ali knew he was right. From the looks of the horses, a strong Nevada wind would blow them away.

Jamie looked Ali straight in the eye. "If you want to help these horses, you've got to know beyond a doubt that you can do it," he said. "It's a tough job, no doubt about it. In some of the cases my dad worked on, the horses were too weak to regain their health. Sometimes the refeeding program causes problems. Sometimes they die."

Sometimes they die. If she started to care for these horses and they died, could she handle it? Probably not. She was still trying to deal with Max dying. Ali tried to put it out of her mind and think about the other things Jamie had mentioned instead. "What's a refeeding program?"

Her parents and Dr. Forrester arrived back at the corrals just as Ali asked the question.

45

"It's the nutrition plan for starved horses," the vet explained. "It takes a while to get them back to their normal feed programs and a healthy weight."

Ali drew her brows together. "You'd think just putting a lot of food in front of them would work."

"That works for a horse that's just down on its weight or has maybe missed a couple of meals," the vet said. "But these horses have gone days without eating, on top of already losing a lot of their body weight over a short period of time. Giving them a lot of food at once, especially the wrong kind of food, could lead to a condition called refeeding syndrome. That can cause kidney, heart, or respiratory failure. They could die."

Ali stared at the horses again. They stood with heads down and ears not moving, despite the human voices and birdcalls around them. Maybe she could at least nurse them back to health so someone else could give them love and attention and a good home. "Do you really think I can help save them?"

"My dad has a plan to save these horses," Jamie said.

His father nodded. "I believe it can be done. The question you have to ask yourself is whether or not *you* can do the work."

"I don't know you that well, Ali," Jamie continued. "I *do* know that you like to step on toes. But I don't really have any idea what you're capable of."

Ali smiled despite herself. Her mom elbowed her dad in the ribs and gave him a knowing smile. Did they think she had a crush on this boy? She didn't.

Jamie gave her a crooked grin. "But something tells me, Ali McCormick, that you're totally up to this. I think there's a big part of you that *wants* to do it. And me and my dad, plus your parents, will be here to help."

"It's a big project, Ali," her mother said. "Maybe more than we really thought about in our haste to help these horses. But your father and I both believe you're capable of doing this, and we're here to help any way we can."

Ali tried to sort out the thoughts that were kickboxing each other in her mind. *Do I want to do this? Or do I want someone else to take on this problem?* Having Jamie standing so close to her didn't help her thought process at all. She gathered her courage. "Okay," she said. "I can do it. Let's save these horses."

She smiled and so did everyone else. Underneath, she was quaking in her shoes. Her parents, Jamie, and the vet had a lot of confidence in her. But her own doubts were as big as the blue Nevada sky above them.

Eight

I was hoping you'd agree to help." Dr. Forrester patted her on the back. "We've got a lot of ground to cover. Why don't you take notes?" He handed her his clipboard.

Jamie pulled a flake of alfalfa hay from the back of the truck. Ali could see several bales of the bright, leafy hay stacked there. She knew that each bale weighed about eighty pounds; when opened, it would flake into about fourteen little sections, making it easier to feed the horses.

"I thought alfalfa was really high in protein. Won't it be hard for the horses to digest?" Ali asked. "Seems like plain ol' grass hay would be easier on their stomachs."

"Actually, that's a really good question," Dr. Forrester said. "It's one of the big mistakes people make when they try to rehab a starved horse. There are a lot of scientific studies, but I'll give you the short version. Basically, a starved horse isn't used to having food in its system, so you can't just throw them back into a regular routine. They can't handle it and their body will rebel."

"Is that refeeding syndrome?" Ali asked.

"Good memory!" Jamie said. He handed the flake of alfalfa to his dad.

"Alfalfa is high in nutrients and low in the sugars and starches that are in most grass hays and grains." The vet pulled two feed buckets from the bed of the truck and set them on the ground. "A starved horse's body can't handle all those carbohydrates from grass hay or grain rations."

Ali thought back to the night she and Cara had snuck onto Mrs. Marshall's property. Thank goodness they hadn't found any feed in the barn. If they *had* found a bag of grain or a bale of hay... "What exactly happens?" she asked.

"The sudden overload of carbohydrates can cause a depletion of electrolytes in the horse's system," he continued. "And that can lead to death by heart, respiratory, or kidney failure a few days after the initial feeding."

Ali shuddered. "Why...how does that happen?"

"When an animal—even a human—has been starved, its body starts using fat deposits that have been stored in reserve," Dr. Forrester explained. "When there aren't any more fat reserves to use, the body resorts to stealing protein from the heart, muscles, and intestines to keep the animal alive."

"Maybe that's why the white mare is a little better off than the gelding?" Ali asked. "She used to be a lot fatter than him."

"You're probably right about that," Jamie agreed. "That could explain the difference in their health."

The vet broke up the alfalfa flake into quarters. "Okay, here's what all of you need to know about their feed. We're going to keep the horses in separate pens so we can keep track of exactly how much each is eating. For the first three days, they'll need small portions every four hours, around the clock."

"You divided it up into such small portions," Ali's mom said. "It looks like it's barely enough to feed a mouse, let alone a full-grown horse. How many of those sections does each horse get?"

Dr. Forrester shook one of them into a feed bucket. "Just one of these small sections per horse, every four hours, for three days. Understand?"

Ali looked at the small amount of food in each bucket. "I don't think this would even fill *me* up."

"It's a feast compared to what they've been getting." Jamie picked up the halter, buckled it over the white mare's head, and led her into the next pen.

The vet continued with his instructions. "On days four through seven, we're going to up their feed to a whole flake of alfalfa per horse, but we're going to stretch the feedings out to every eight hours instead of every four."

"That's a little better," Ali's dad said as Ali scribbled furiously, afraid she might miss something.

Dr. Forrester handed her father one of the buckets. "On week two, we'll up the hay intake just a little more. By the end of that week, we should be able to feed them as much as they want to eat. At that point, their energy levels should be coming up. You should notice a lot more movement of their ears, eyes, and heads. Right now, these poor animals are in such bad shape that they don't really have much interest in anything."

Ali took the bucket from her father and squeezed through the fence into the gelding's pen. Quietly she approached the scrawny animal, speaking softly so as not to startle him. "Hey, big guy." She held out the bucket of sweet-smelling alfalfa and waited for several moments, but the gelding just stood there, his ears out to the sides and his bottom lip drooping. His eyes looked distant and glazed, like he didn't even know she was there.

Memories of Max flashed across her mind. This horse was

just a bigger version of her pony. The pony she had loved and couldn't save.

She lowered the bucket and backed up several steps. Her shoulders slumped. *I shouldn't have volunteered for this. I can't do it.* She put the feed bucket down.

"What's the matter?" Jamie asked.

Ali had been so wrapped up in the gelding's sad eyes that she had forgotten Jamie was there. She turned back to look at the horse and her chest felt like it was caving in, crushing her heart. *I can't do this.* She would have to tell everyone she'd changed her mind. They'd have to find someone else to care for the Appaloosas. Maybe Cara could do it? She'd love working with Jamie and his dad.

"What's wrong?" Jamie asked again. He set his bucket on the ground and the mare poked her head into it, nibbling at the hay and chewing slowly.

Her father entered the pen. "Ali, honey, are you okay?"

Ali crossed her arms and avoided looking at them all. "He won't eat," she mumbled. "He's probably going to die."

"Whoa, hold on there." Jamie moved closer, forcing her to look at him. "Things might seem a little bleak at this moment, but how about a little optimism here? Let's give this horse a chance."

Ali turned her face away and dragged the back of her hand across her eyes.

"Are you crying?" Jamie asked.

"No," Ali said, but she was pretty sure there were traces left on her cheeks.

"Look, Ali," Dr. Forrester said. "I know this is hard. It's always difficult to deal with situations like this—especially after what you went through with your pony. But we're doing a really important thing here."

Ali avoided everyone's gaze. "I already lost one horse," she murmured. "I don't want to take a chance on another."

Ali's dad patted the black Appy on the neck. "Look, honey, I know this is rough on you. But these horses are here and they need help. You've just got to have a little faith and determination. Your mother and I wouldn't have brought them home if we didn't think we could do this. You've got a special way with horses; you seem to have forgotten how good you were with Max."

Jamie picked up the gelding's bucket and held it out for Ali. "Come on, let me show you how to convince this guy that he needs to eat this really tasty hay."

Ali looked at the two abused horses. She wanted to turn away and pretend they didn't exist, pretend she didn't see Max every time she looked at the black gelding. But she couldn't leave the sad scene before her, couldn't ignore their blank, hopeless stares. Her heart ached for them. They needed someone to care for them. Someone who wouldn't let them down like their owner had.

Her hand tightened on the feed bucket. Her father was right. These horses desperately needed help. She couldn't bring Max back, but she *could* give this gelding and mare a second chance at life. It didn't mean that she had to keep them, or fall in love with them. She could help make them well so that someone else could adopt them.

She took a deep breath and looked Jamie in the eye. "Okay, I'm ready to try again," she said, embarrassed that she'd given up so easily a few moments ago. *This time,* she promised herself, *I won't give up.*

Nine

Jamie took a small handful of the alfalfa and crushed the delicate green leaves and stems in his hand. Ali watched as he gently inserted a portion into the place at the side of the gelding's mouth where horses have no teeth, then massaged his cheeks. The black horse moved his lips a bit, then rolled the alfalfa flakes around on his tongue.

"That a boy," Jamie said encouragingly.

"I think he's getting the idea." Her mother looked relieved. "Can Ali try?"

Jamie motioned her closer and handed her some crushed leaves. Ali's fingers were shaking as she inserted them into the gelding's mouth.

"Be careful, Ali," her father warned. "That horse has really big teeth and they're about an inch from your fingers."

Ali moved her hands to the horse's jaw, remembering when she'd gotten her finger pinched trying to put the bit in Max's mouth. It definitely hurt, and she didn't want to repeat the experience. She rubbed the gelding's cheeks and lips in an effort to get him to chew. She heard a grinding sound as his jaws worked back and forth a couple of times and her hopes climbed a notch. It would take them all day to get that food eaten at this pace. But it was a start.

Ali and her parents waved goodbye to Jamie and Dr. Forrester as they drove away. They had finally gotten the gelding to eat most of his ration. Now he stood with his head down and ears out to the side, looking more like a mule than a horse.

The mare was a lot more alert than the gelding. She had licked the bucket clean and seemed to be hoping for more. Her ears moved back and forth at the sound of their voices.

"I know you're a bit ambivalent about this project," her mother said, "but we think it's the right thing to do. You didn't mean to start this when you trespassed, but we're going to finish it by getting these horses back into shape."

Ali's dad clapped her on the back. "It looks like you're up to this task. We're willing to pitch in when needed, and we'll keep an eye on things, but this project is mainly yours. Do you understand?"

Ali nodded. Not that long ago, she had considered caring for horses to be the best job in the world. But now, with everything that had happened, it seemed like punishment—and it was, for breaking her parents' rules.

She picked up the buckets and stacked them where Jamie had unloaded the bales. It hurt to be near horses, but she'd try to be strong and get through this. The horses deserved that much.

She had Dr. Forrester's cell number in her pocket. He'd promised to return in the morning. That made her feel a lot better, but for now, Ali was on her own.

Cara was going to be so shocked. If only she could be here to help. Cara knew a lot about horses. Ali did too, but she didn't completely trust herself right now. She didn't want to make any mistakes.

"So, what are you going to name them?" Her mother leaned over the fence and scratched the white mare on the shoulder.

"Don't they already have names?" Ali asked. "Mrs. Marshall had these horses for years."

Her father shrugged. "Mrs. Marshall didn't tell anyone their names," he said. "I hear she's going to be moving to California to live with her son. The poor old woman has enough to deal with right now with her memory loss and all."

"Besides," her mother added, "I think it would be best if these guys started with a clean slate. They've got a new home and a new chance at life; I think they should start it with new names too."

"I don't need to pick out names," Ali said, shaking her head. "They won't be here long. I'll just help them get better, then when someone adopts them, they'll name them."

"But, dear…," her mother began. "They need names. You can't just say Horse Number One and Horse Number Two."

Ali's dad put his arm around his wife. "I guess that'll be okay for now, Ali. Once the horses are better, we'll talk about it again."

Ali heard hoofbeats. Cara rode up the driveway on her quarter horse gelding. His registered name was something fancy, but the little brown bay with the black mane and tail was so chubby that Cara had nicknamed him Dumpling.

Cara's mouth dropped open at the sight of the horses. "Wow!"

"Have you come to see our new additions?" Ali's mom asked.

"No, ma'am, I didn't know they were here." Cara dismounted and pulled Dumpling's reins over his head, leading him toward Ali's parents. "I came to see you and Mr. McCormick."

What? Now it was Ali's turn for a jaw-dropping reaction.

Cara stood tall, her head bowed. "I want to apologize for getting Ali into trouble the other night."

"That's good of you, Cara," Ali's dad said. "But the choice was as much Ali's fault as yours. It was her decision to go with you."

"Ali is thirteen," her mom added. "That's plenty old enough to know right from wrong. She made the bad decision to go along with *your* bad decision." Her tone softened. "But I'm proud of you, Cara, for having the nerve to come over and try to make things right."

Cara is *brave,* Ali thought. Hopefully some of that courage would rub off on her.

"I just feel bad about instigating the whole thing. It was a dangerous thing to do." Cara fussed with Dumpling's reins. "But I knew those horses were in a lot of trouble and I just had to see for myself. I know Ali was worried too." She shoved her hair behind her ears. "I just wanted to tell you I'm sorry I got Ali into trouble."

"Well, Cara, that's very mature of you," Ali's dad said. "We appreciate it. Ali is still grounded from going places with you this week, but you're welcome to come here and help out with the horses if you'd like."

Ali's mom smiled sadly. "I think our daughter has forgotten how good she is with horses. She could use a little help finding her way with them again, Cara."

Ali's parents walked back to the house, leaving the girls alone.

Cara opened the gate to one of the empty corrals and led Dumpling inside, removing his bridle and loosening his saddle. "See...I'm learning some good things from you," she said. "A little while ago, I would have never thought about apologizing to someone else's parents. It's scary! But I guess it did some good, because now they're going to let me come over and help."

Dumpling went to the fence and poked his head over the rail, nickering to the newcomers. The white mare turned her head slightly, but the gelding didn't even seem to notice.

Cara pulled two red licorice vines from her saddlebag. She picked a few horse hairs off of them and handed one to Ali. They tapped their pieces of candy in a toast, then took big bites. "Now tell me how in the world all this happened," Cara said.

Ali shrugged. "As far as I can tell, this is my punishment for trespassing. Plus, I think my parents have this crazy idea that if I take care of these horses, I'll want one again."

"Would that really be such a terrible thing?" Cara asked softly. "Horses are so awesome! I know you've made yourself some kind of crazy promise not to ever like them again, but *never* is a long, long time, Ali. Think of all you're missing."

Ali rested her chin on the top rail of the corral. She remembered riding across the desert, Max's mane blowing in her face. It had been so much fun! "Maybe someday," she said. "I'm just not ready yet."

"I'd say it's a little too late for that."

Ali pursed her lips. "It wasn't fair of my parents to do this without asking me first."

"*Fair-schmair,*" Cara said. "Your parents are pretty cool. I'm sure they did what they thought was best. Just think...if you had a full-grown horse instead of a pony, you might stand a chance of beating me and Dumpling."

Ali couldn't help smiling. "Max couldn't help it if he was short!"

She felt a nibble on her elbow and turned to look into the

kind eyes of the white mare. The horse lipped her shirt, begging for attention.

Ali reached out hesitantly and stroked the mare's muzzle. Both horses had the mottled spotting and striped hooves that Appaloosas were known for. At the peak of their health, they had been beautiful examples of the breed. It pained her to see them as they were now.

"You won't believe how little their meals are," she told Cara. "They get a quarter-flake of alfalfa every four hours. That's it."

"You're kidding!" Cara said. "Dumpling would eat that in three bites. Why so little?"

Ali filled her in on all the details of the horses' special care. "Oh, no!" Cara gasped. "Imagine if we'd found any food in the barn that night.... We might have caused serious harm."

"I'm still afraid I'll make a mistake that's going to hurt them," Ali admitted. "Especially the black horse. He's a lot worse off." She picked at a stem of hay and broke it into several pieces, letting them drift to the ground. "The vet says there's a chance he might not make it."

"And you don't want to go through that again with the horse that looks just like Max?"

"Yup." Ali pushed away from the fence and shoved her hands into her pockets.

"My dad says that animals can't always help themselves," Cara said. "So sometimes we have to forget about what *we* want and do what's best for them. You did what was best for Max, Ali. Quit beating yourself up over it. A break that bad is a death sentence for a horse. You know that. Look how they spent millions when that famous racehorse broke his leg a few years ago. He had the best veterinary care anyone could buy, and they still couldn't save him."

Cara was probably right, but it didn't matter. Ali still felt horrible. She cleared her throat and changed the subject. "These horses don't even have names. Mrs. Marshall didn't tell anyone what she called them."

"Then let's name them!" Cara said. "They've got to have names. What do you want to call the black gelding?"

Ali studied the horse, remembering how strong and proud he had been before he was neglected. Maybe it wouldn't hurt to give him a name? It didn't mean she was keeping them or anything. "He needs a strong name," she said. "Something that goes along with his Appaloosa heritage."

"Well, the Nez Perce Indians developed the breed a few hundred years ago," Cara said. "Maybe you should pick something that shows that cool lineage."

"Yeah!" Ali said. "When I got Max, I read up on Appaloosas. There are *cave* paintings in France that show spotted horses. Scientists said they date back to 18,000 BC!"

"I remember when this guy used to run across Mrs. Marshall's paddock, with the wind cutting across it," Cara said, patting the black horse. "Bucking and kicking, with his mane waving in the breeze. Like he was dancing."

"I hope he'll be able to do that again someday soon," Ali said. "Maybe we should call him Wind Dancer."

"That's a good name!"

Ali entered the gelding's pen and stood beside him. He didn't even acknowledge her. She reached out to finger-comb his thin mane, but he still didn't react. In a way, it was probably good that he wasn't friendly. It would make it easier to find another home for him once he was well again.

"Can I name the mare?" Cara asked.

"Only if you promise not to name her something silly like Muffin, or Cupcake, or *Dumpling*."

Cara rolled her eyes. "Dumpling is a perfectly good name. And he lives up to it too." She studied the white mare for moment, then declared, "I think we should call her Misty."

"Misty." Ali liked the sound of it. "Misty it is!"

The white mare wanted more attention, so Ali joined Cara on the top rail of the fence. Misty stood with her head between them for several minutes while Cara petted her. Ali gave the mare a couple of strokes. After a bit, Misty went to the other end of the pen to lie down.

"Oh, I almost forgot to tell you," Ali said. "Jamie helped deliver the horses. He's working with his dad. He'll be here every day for a while."

"Wooo-hooo!" Cara hollered. "Bonus! You can count on me to be here too."

Ali felt a momentary twinge of jealousy, but she shook it off with a laugh. Of course Cara wanted to hang out with a cute boy.

"I'm going to head up to the house," Ali said. "I want to tell my parents the horses' names, and I need to finish my homework now. These around-the-clock feedings are going to really eat into my free time. It's a good thing we're out of school in a few days."

"Yeah, I can't wait!" Cara picked up Dumpling's bridle and went to his pen to ready him for the ride home. She tightened the girth on the saddle, then glanced sideways at Ali. "I know you're upset about your mom and dad bringing these horses home, but I'm glad they did. I think it's all going to work out." She slid her boot into the stirrup and swung aboard, then waved goodbye and trotted down the drive.

Ali watched them go, Dumpling's big hindquarters swaying as they disappeared around the corner.

She walked up the back porch steps and kicked off her shoes. As she turned the doorknob, she heard raised voices inside the house. Danny stood by the staircase, his crutches under his arms; their father faced him, holding his prosthetic.

"Son, you're never going to get used to this thing unless you wear it," their dad said. "There's a good Veteran's Hospital in town. We can make you an appointment with them if you think it will help."

"I don't need it, and I'm not going to wear it!" Danny hollered. "And for the hundredth time, I'm not going to the VA. I don't need any help! Why can't you guys just leave me alone?"

Ali ducked back into the kitchen. If they spotted her, she'd be sent to her room, and she wanted to hear this conversation.

"Danny, honey..." Their mom stepped into the fray. "You need to get out and start doing things again. When you first got home, you went out for a drive with your friends a couple of times. You seemed to enjoy it. What changed?" She sounded exasperated. "And why don't you want to wear your prosthetic?"

"I just don't want to, okay?" Danny snapped. "Let's just let it drop." He turned on his crutches and started toward the staircase.

"Just a minute, son," his dad said. "There's one other thing I'd like to ask of you."

Ali moved closer to the doorway to hear better.

"Would you take your sister to the feed store? She needs to buy supplies for the horses. I'm sure you saw them delivered this morning. And your sister would enjoy spending more time with you."

Ali gulped. Now she was getting dragged into this. But if it would get him out of the house, she'd ride to town with her grouchy brother.

"It's only a few miles away," their mother coaxed. "I know you can do this, Danny. Please take your sister to the feed store. It'll be good for both of you."

Danny frowned but he stuck out his hand for the keys.

Their mom deposited the keys into his palm. "It's time to get back into a normal routine around here." She kissed her son on the cheek. "It's a nice day out. It'll be good for you to get out in the fresh air."

Ali's dad placed the prosthetic on the couch. "I appreciate it, Danny. I know dealing with this injury is hard on you."

Danny grunted and made his way to the couch. He snatched the prosthetic leg off the cushion, then maneuvered to put it on.

Ali leaned against the wall, waiting for her brother to put on his fake leg. The part of the prosthetic that attached to his knee was flesh-colored, but the piece leading down to the foot was shiny metal. For some odd reason, she was fascinated by the foot portion, which was encased in one of Danny's sneakers. She guessed it was to make the unit look as normal as possible. But what if he wanted to wear another pair of shoes and he forgot to change the shoe on the prosthetic? He'd have two mismatched shoes.

"Quit staring at me, Ali." Danny didn't even bother to look at her.

She'd thought she was out of his line of vision. And now her parents would know that she'd been eavesdropping.

Ali headed toward the stairs, wanting to get out of there before her parents lectured her on listening to other people's private conversations. "I'll go change my clothes and be down in a minute," she said.

She took the stairs two at a time. She was actually surprised that Danny had agreed to take her. She'd have Danny all to herself for at least thirty minutes. Maybe they'd have a good time and he'd remember that she wasn't so bad after all.

Ten

The screen door banged shut and Ali watched from the truck's passenger seat as Danny cautiously made his way down the steps, wearing his new prosthetic and using a cane to help him balance. His gait was awkward and unsure. Ali wanted to get out of the truck and help him, but she knew he wouldn't want her to.

He folded his long body behind the steering wheel and sat there for several moments. He turned on the radio and fussed with it for a bit, then adjusted all the mirrors and his seat.

Danny tapped his fingers and whistled along with the tune on the radio. She hadn't heard her brother whistle in many years. Was he stalling, hoping their father would volunteer to drive them?

Ali picked at her nails while she waited, feeling awkward. Finally Danny handed her a list and some cash.

"Mom says this is what the vet suggested you get at the feed store." He fidgeted with the rearview mirror again. "She said you'd know what to pick out for brushes and such." He cracked his knuckles and put the truck in drive, slowly pulling to the end of the driveway. "Make sure your seat belt is on," he ordered, then softened his voice. "You can never be too careful."

"Especially when we're in our own driveway." There was a long unsettling pause and she began to regret her attempt at humor, then Danny burst out laughing. It was the first real laugh she'd heard from him since he'd come home.

"Are you going to be okay driving with your new leg?" she asked. "Are you worried?"

"Nah, I've driven a couple times since I've been home. This truck's an automatic. I can use my good right leg for the gas and brake." He reached over and tugged on a lock of her hair, like he used to do when they were kids, then pulled out onto the road.

Ali was relieved she didn't have to worry about coming up with stuff to talk about; he had the radio up too loud for them to hear each other.

They came to the small stretch of freeway on the way to the feed store. As they merged into traffic, Danny's demeanor changed. He sat up straighter and his eyes darted all around. He watched his mirrors constantly and seemed overly anxious when cars pulled alongside them or passed.

She didn't remember him ever being this cautious when he was younger. He'd been a little bit of a daredevil before he'd left for the war. Maybe the Army had taught him a different driving technique?

And then it dawned on her. Danny had had to be vigilant all the time when he was in Afghanistan—if he wanted to stay alive.

She swallowed hard, knowing she couldn't imagine what it would be like to live in a war zone every day. She found it difficult to be around horses after what she'd gone through with Max, but that was nothing compared to what Danny had experienced.

She had healed; her arm was back to normal. Danny

would never get his leg back—or his peace of mind, it seemed. *Poor Danny.*

Ali stared down the road ahead of them. Hot tears pressed against the backs of her eyes, but she didn't dare cry in front of Danny.

"Hey, why the long face?" Danny hollered over the music. "You've got two horses standing in the corrals. You should be happy as a crow in a cornfield. You get a chance to start all over again. I think that's great."

Ali shrugged. "Cara and I named them," she said. "At least for now. The black gelding is Wind Dancer, and the white mare is Misty."

"Good names."

And that was where the conversation stopped. Ali was actually kind of glad. She didn't want to talk about horses anymore.

A few minutes later, they pulled into the parking lot of Smith's Feed Store. Ali climbed out of the truck and closed the door. Danny didn't make any move to follow her, so she poked her head back through the window and asked, "Are you coming in?"

"Unless you need my help, I'll just wait here and listen to music. I don't really have any interest in looking at horse stuff."

"I'll be done in about ten minutes." Ali turned to leave.

"Wait." He held a twenty-dollar bill out the window. "Buy something for yourself, okay? Get something special that you wouldn't normally spend your own money on."

Ali hesitated, but took the money when he poked it at her. This must be his way of apologizing for the way he'd been behaving. "Thanks," she said, and tried to smile.

Smith's Feed Store was cool and inviting inside. It had

been a long time since she'd been here. She stood in the corner and closed her eyes, taking in the smell of hay, oats, and
saddle leather. It was one of the best smelling places on earth.

In the other room Ali could hear the *peep, peep, peep* of baby
chicks and the soft mumble of people talking. She opened
her eyes and looked around. The owner had moved things
around since she'd last shopped here.

She selected a rubber curry comb, a soft body brush, and a
hoof pick, then ordered a couple of bales of alfalfa at the
counter. The horses weren't allowed to eat much right now, so
there was no sense in buying much more. Besides, once they
were allowed to eat normal rations, they would switch back to
grass hay. Horses that weren't being worked hard didn't really
need the high protein that alfalfa provided.

"Can I please get a bag of grain too?" she asked. She
hoped the horses would be ready for it soon. Max had loved
grain. It was his favorite, besides carrots.

She paid for it all, then remembered the money that
Danny had given her. What could she buy? She didn't want
to purchase any tack, not that there was any available for
twenty dollars.

The peeping of the chicks drew her attention again. Ali
walked over to the cage. She couldn't help smiling when she
looked at the cute little yellow balls of fluff. They meandered
around the cage, pecking at their food and the pine shavings
on the floor.

"How much for two chicks?" Ali asked. "And what would I
need to go with them?"

Ten minutes later, she left the feed store with several bags
and a small box with holes punched in the lid. Danny
frowned when he heard the peeps. "Is that what my twenty
dollars bought?"

She nodded. "There's one for me and one for you, and they're really, really cute."

Danny smacked his palm to his forehead. "And we're *really, really* going to be in trouble when Mom and Dad see us hop out of the truck with an armload of baby chicks."

"The feed guy says they're both girls," Ali said. "I didn't think the neighbors would like to hear a rooster waking them up at dawn."

The truck rocked as the loading boys tossed the bales of alfalfa and sack of grain into the back. When they were done, Danny started the engine. "I don't think our family would appreciate it much either," he said. "But Mom's really good at frying chicken."

"Ugh!" Ali pulled the box of chicks closer. "Not funny, brother." But she chuckled anyway. "I think we should name them. I'm going to call mine Henrietta. Henrietta the Hen. What are you going to call yours?" She opened the box and tilted it so Danny could see inside. "It's the one with the little dark spot on its head."

"I'm not naming a stupid chicken." He pulled forward and they waited at the edge of the parking lot while an old beater car rolled past them, sputtering and belching smoke. Danny pulled carefully onto the road behind it and headed toward the four-lane highway. The smoke from the vehicle floated into the open windows of their truck.

"Just our luck." Ali fanned the air. "Can we go around this guy? This smoke is horrible."

Danny eyed all of his mirrors. "We'll be on the highway soon. It's only a short drive to our exit. I don't want to drive any faster. The speed limit is only twenty-five here."

Ali stretched her T-shirt up over her nose and counted the mileage markers until they came to the exit. Danny steered the truck to the right to make the ramp and sped up just a bit to get out of the cloud of smoke.

Suddenly the old car backfired. *Kaboom!*

Danny screamed and jerked the steering wheel hard left. Ali grabbed the dashboard as the truck careened out of control, fishtailing wildly.

"Roll over, roll over!" Danny hollered as he tried to gain control of the truck. "Heads down!"

Everything seemed to move in slow motion. The truck spun in a circle but stayed upright, heading toward a patch of desert at the side of the road. The tires screeched and the truck came to rest against the sagebrush in the deep sand.

The chicks peeped loudly; their box had landed upside-down near the door. Ali reached for it and held it tight to her chest, trying hard not to blubber.

Danny sat with his hands gripping the steering wheel, staring blindly out the window. Slowly he turned to face her, his eyes still clouded and distant, like he didn't know where he was. Her hiccupping cries must have cut through the murk because Ali could see him gradually begin to focus. The guilt and fear that flashed across his face squeezed her heart.

He reached across the seat and pulled her into a protective hug. The seat belt held her in place, straining against her neck. She thought she might suffocate. The chicks protested loudly as the pressure against their small box mounted.

Danny finally released her, but then he took her face in his shaking hands. "Are you okay, sis? Ali, are you hurt?"

It had been a long time since she'd heard that much concern in her brother's voice. She shook her head, but tears still streamed down her cheeks. She couldn't help it. It wasn't the accident—it was Danny. He still had a faraway look in his eyes. It scared her.

Danny checked her for blood or cuts, clumsily turning her head and accidently pulling her hair.

"I'm fine!" Ali said as loudly as she could. "I'm okay," she repeated in a calmer voice and pulled away.

Danny stared out the window and scrubbed his face with his trembling hands. "We're gonna be okay," he whispered. "Everything is fine."

Ali set the baby chicks on the seat beside her. At the moment, it didn't feel like things would ever be okay again.

Eleven

Ali couldn't stop shaking. "Are you okay?" she asked Danny. "What happened back there?"

"I don't know," he said. "I was driving down the road, and next thing I know, we're swerving all over the place. We're lucky we didn't crash. What happened? Did we blow a tire or something?"

"That old car backfired and you hollered and pulled on the wheel," she reminded him. "The truck started spinning out of control, and we ended up here."

"What backfire? I remember passing the old car as we entered the ramp..." Danny paused, rubbing his temples. "Wait...there was a loud noise before we skidded off the ramp."

"Danny, are you sure you're okay?" Ali tried to keep the worry out of her voice. Maybe she should call her parents? She looked around for her cell phone, but it had been flung somewhere in the truck when they were spinning.

"Why does everyone keep asking me that?" he asked. *"I'm fine!"*

A car passed, slowing down to take a look at the truck

wedged in the sagebrush. Ali could see the kids in the back staring out the window, their mouths agape.

Danny put the truck in gear and gave it some gas. The tires spun a few times then took hold, and the truck crawled back onto the ramp. He glanced at Ali. "When we get home…"

"Yeah, I know the routine," Ali said, sounding snarkier than she intended. "Don't tell Mom and Dad because you don't want to upset them."

Danny didn't respond. Instead, he glanced back into the bed of the truck. "At least we didn't lose any of the feed."

The chicks started peeping again and Ali pulled the box onto her lap. "Do you think Mom and Dad will let me keep them?" she asked, trying to change the subject.

Danny kept his eyes on the road. He seemed a little more relaxed and his voice was softer. "I don't know. The family could probably use a pet. But I'm not really sure if chickens qualify."

Ten minutes later, they pulled into the driveway. Danny drove around to the back and parked near the barn. Misty watched them pull up, but Wind Dancer stood with his head down, seemingly oblivious to anything that went on around him.

Their parents were waiting in the yard. *Great*, Ali thought. How could she get out of the truck and act as if nothing had happened?

She opened the door and hopped down, holding the box of chicks. She glanced at the truck. She noticed some light scratches on the side panel from the sagebrush, but there was no other damage.

"What have you got there?" Her father dropped the tailgate and started unloading the feed.

Ali hesitated, but Danny jumped right in. "I bought Ali a couple of baby chicks." He set the bags of supplies down next to the corral. "Thought it might be nice to have some fresh eggs for breakfast sometime in the near future." He winked at Ali.

Ali's heart swelled. She vowed not to give up on him.

"Hmmm…" Her mother inspected the new additions. A chick peeped and she smiled. "I'm not sure where we should put them. There's no chicken coop here and you can't let them roam the yard when they're this little. Stray cats, hawks, or coyotes would get them."

"I didn't think about that," Ali said. "Maybe I can keep them in my room?"

Her dad stacked the bales of hay on the pallet next to the corrals and set down the grain beside them. "Chickens aren't indoor pets, Ali. But I saw some chicken wire in the back of the barn. We can dig through that pile of old boards to find something you can use."

"Maybe your brother can help?" their mom suggested.

Danny limped toward the house. "Maybe later, Mom. I'm really tired. The trip wore me out and this prosthetic is hurting me."

"It's okay." Ali put the box of chicks on top of the hay bales. "I can probably come up with something."

"I'll help you put it together," her father offered.

Some of Danny's stubbornness must have rubbed off on her. "Thanks, Dad, but I can do this myself," she said. "How hard can it be to build a pen for a couple of tiny chicks?"

But two hours later when she stood back and looked at her new chicken pen, she had to admit that she might be the new slumlord of Chickenville. The posts were crooked and the wire wasn't secured to them very well. She had no idea how to build a coop, so she'd given up and used an empty cardboard box with a blanket inside.

Cara rode up. "What is it?" she asked, staring at the mess.

Ali sighed. "It's a chicken pen for the new chicks I bought."

"Can I see them?"

Ali opened the cardboard box and Cara scooped out one of the chicks, holding it close and rubbing her chin against its soft, fuzzy feathers.

"That one is Henrietta," Ali said. "Danny hasn't named his yet."

"One of these is Danny's?" Cara asked. "I thought he just hung out in his room all day playing video games. He doesn't seem the baby-chick-type guy."

"He's not. But I'm trying to get him interested in *something* and I thought maybe he'd like a pet."

"Chickens aren't really pets." Cara scratched the chick's head. "I mean, they're cute when they're this size. But you can't really *do* anything with them. They grow up into chickens and just kind of strut around the yard and lay eggs. *Booooring!*"

They set the chicks loose in their pen and watched as they pecked at the feed and stumbled into their water dish. Their little peeps were comforting.

It had been almost two years since Ali had had a pet. It felt kind of good to have one again. Of course, there were the horses. But they were just here temporarily. As soon as they got better, someone else would adopt them. Ali glanced at her cell phone. "It's time to feed the horses."

She cut open the top bale of hay and separated the flake of alfalfa into quarters. She shook a quarter flake into each bucket and handed one to her friend. Cara went straight for Misty's pen, leaving her to feed the black gelding. Had her friend done that on purpose, forcing her to spend more time with Wind Dancer? *Well, it won't work,* she thought. *I'm not going to fall in love with these horses.*

She let herself into the other pen and offered the hay to Wind Dancer. Once again he showed little interest. Ali noticed that Misty walked right up to Cara and stuck her head into the feed bucket. She wished Wind Dancer would do the same. Maybe she was doing something wrong.

She tried to remember what Jamie had shown her. She crushed some of the alfalfa leaves in her hand then rubbed them near his nostrils to give him the scent. Next, she put some of the soft pieces in his mouth, gently pushing them through the space at the side.

Wind Dancer rolled those around on his tongue for a bit. Ali gave him some more, being careful to leave out the stems for the moment. The gelding worked those back into his grinder teeth at the back of his jaw and Ali felt the thrill of victory when he started to chew. She gave him another mouthful and waited for him to chew it. It seemed like it took forever.

"Misty is done." Cara presented the empty bucket. "Are you sure we can't give her just a little more?"

Ali looked up in surprise. She had been concentrating so hard on Wind Dancer that she had forgotten about Misty and Cara. She shook her head vehemently. "Dr. Forrester said no. I don't know where the dividing line is on too much food. I don't want to take a chance on overfeeding them. It might make them sick."

"Yeah, I guess you're right," Cara said. "Better to be safe."

Ali held the bucket while Wind Dancer picked through the hay, chewing slowly. She remembered what he had looked like when he was healthy: broad-chested, with a compact body and large hindquarters. His legs were still strong and straight—like most Appys—but he didn't show much desire to use them.

She had to smile when she looked at his wispy mane and tail. Misty's was the same way. Most Appaloosas didn't have long, thick manes and tails like other horses. Max's had been pretty sparse too.

Her heart pinched a little when she thought of her pony. Try as she might to forget those fun times she missed so badly, she just couldn't. But today, when she was standing here staring at a larger version of Max, it didn't seem to hurt quite so much.

The gelding ate a little more food, but he still had about a quarter of his ration left. At least he seemed to be improving. Maybe in another four hours, when it was time for the next feeding, he would eat the entire portion. She clipped the feed pail to the railing in case he decided he wanted to finish it off. The vet hadn't mentioned any time limit.

"Can we brush them?" Cara asked. "You seem to be getting along pretty well with Wind Dancer. I bet he'd enjoy it."

Ali shook her head. "Not today." She'd come too close to feeling something for Wind Dancer just a moment ago. She didn't want to take the chance of brushing and fussing over the horses and possibly bonding with them. Their coats were clean enough for now.

Cara gave her a strange look, but Ali shrugged it off. "Jamie washed and brushed them before they brought them over."

"Okay." Cara didn't sound convinced. "Then I'll head home and do some homework."

"Wow, I'm impressed!" Ali slapped her a high five. "I really am rubbing off on you."

Cara picked up her bike. "Just don't tell anyone. I don't

want to wreck my reputation as a wild child," she said with a laugh.

"You're smart." Ali walked down the driveway with Cara. "You could get better grades if you'd just study. And you know I'll help you anytime you need it."

"Thanks." Cara swung her leg over her bicycle. "Maybe you can help me study, and I'll help you with the horses."

"Deal!" Ali waved goodbye, then walked up her back steps and headed to her room. Grabbing her books, she took a seat at her desk by the window.

She tried to focus on her homework, but her eyes kept drifting to the horses below. What would become of them if she were able to save them? Who would their next owner be? What if it was someone who didn't treat them very well?

Finally it was feed time. Ali jumped out of her chair and made her way to the corrals. Wind Dancer hadn't finished his previous meal, but he had eaten a bit more of it. She gave Misty her ration, knowing that she wouldn't have to coax the mare into eating.

Wind Dancer was another story. She tossed out the small bit he hadn't finished, filled the bucket with fresh hay, and went through the routine again, placing the hay on his tongue and encouraging him to chew. "I think you just want the extra attention," Ali said as she straightened his forelock.

Ali worked with the horse for around an hour. He ate about the same amount as he had earlier, which wasn't much, but at least he was eating. She hung his bucket on the hook and did a quick check on the chicks, then went in to clean up for dinner.

When she came back downstairs, Ali was disappointed to see that Danny wasn't at the table. It had been a crazy day with running off the road and all, but she felt like they had made some progress just hanging out during the ride before that.

When she remembered the spinning truck, her stomach did a rollover. One more secret she had to keep from her parents.

Ali took a seat at the table, praying the guilt didn't show on her face. "Where's Danny?" she asked.

"I think he's sleeping," her mother said. "He can eat when he gets up. I guess the trip to the feed store really wore him out."

Ali groaned inwardly. Her mom had no idea... "So, Cara and I named the horses," she said.

"Oh?" her father said. "And what names did you pick?"

"Please don't tell me Cara chose something like Strudel, or Cupcake!" Her mother laughed.

Ali smiled. "No, we picked good ones," she assured them. "The gelding's name is Wind Dancer, and the mare is Misty."

"Perfect!" her mother said.

After dinner, Ali helped her mom clean up the dishes, then sat down to watch a movie with her dad. The horses' next feeding wouldn't be until 9:00. Her homework was done. She could kick back for a couple of hours and relax.

About halfway through the movie, Ali heard Danny bumping around in the kitchen. He didn't come to join them, so she turned her attention back to the television. When it was over, she got up to go feed the horses and chicks.

"Do you need any help?" her mother asked.

"Thanks, Mom, but I've got it. I just need to go upstairs and change."

The sun was going down, making it difficult to see the barn and corrals, but she peeked out her window while she pulled on her boots. What she saw brought her up short.

Danny was outside. He leaned on the corral by Wind Dancer's pen, his crutches propped against the fence. The gelding pressed his nose against Danny's shirtfront while her brother scratched him behind the ears.

She hurried downstairs and out the back door. "What are you doing?" Her voice sounded harsher than she meant for it to.

Danny's head snapped around in surprise. "Nothing," he mumbled, reaching for his crutches and quickly making his way back to the house.

Ali watched him go, feeling guilty for sounding so accusing. She stared at Wind Dancer. *She* was the one feeding and caring for him. Why didn't he act like he wanted *her* around? It wasn't fair.

She took a deep breath. She should be happy that her brother was interested in something besides video games. And she should be thrilled that Wind Dancer wanted attention— even if it wasn't from her.

She picked up the feed buckets, divided the hay into them, and hung them for the horses to eat. She wasn't sure Wind Dancer would eat his hay on his own, but he needed to start trying. She'd check on him after she fed the baby chicks.

Ali stomped around the corner of the barn, wondering why she felt so peeved. Why should she feel jealous of her brother? It didn't matter who Wind Dancer liked best. She reached the chicken pen and froze.

The pen had been rebuilt. The poles stood straight and the wire was tight. An old doghouse that'd been abandoned behind the barn was serving as a chicken coop; it now housed nesting boxes.

Had her father done this? No, he couldn't have. He'd been watching television with her.

Something lay on the ground next to a hammer. It was Danny's hat. Military issue. The one he had returned home with from Afghanistan.

She felt the lump rise in her throat. Why was everything so upside-down lately? Why couldn't she get things right? She plopped down in the sand beside the rebuilt chicken pen and cried.

Twelve

Ali sat there for a few minutes, feeling sorry for herself. The baby chicks finally brought her out of her pity party. There was barely any light left, but still she could see them hopping around, pecking at the ground, and tumbling over each other.

Danny had cared enough to do something nice for her. Was it his way of apologizing for the accident today? Or did he feel badly about the way he'd behaved since he came home from the war? Whatever it was, she needed to let him know she appreciated his efforts.

Ali changed the chicks' water, added food to their dish, and then wrangled them into the coop for the night. She made her way back to the house to clean up.

After a good scrub down to remove horse hair and chick food, she went to the kitchen and pulled out flour, eggs, butter, sugar, and a bag of chocolate chips.

Ten minutes later her mom came into the kitchen. "What are you up to?" she asked, taking in the mess on the counter and the flour down the front of Ali's shirt. "It's almost your bedtime."

"I'm making cookies for Danny." Ali wiped the spilled

flour off the counter and shook it into the sink. "He fixed my chicken pen while I was watching TV. It looks really good."

Her mom dipped her finger in the cookie dough. "Yum," she said. "Danny will love these. Looks like that ride to the feed store today did you two some good."

"Yes," Ali responded happily. But then she remembered the accident and Danny's bewildered response. "Er…I hope he likes them." Ali tried to steady her voice as she dropped the cookie dough by the spoonful onto the greased cookie sheet. "I've got to get these baked, then try to get a few hours' sleep before the next feeding."

"I'll take over that one," her mother offered. "This project is a little bigger than your father and I realized. You need your sleep. School is almost out and you want to finish strong. You'll have all summer to stay up late."

"No, I can do it, Mom." Ali popped the cookies into the oven. "I guess I'm responsible for them being here, since I turned in Mrs. Marshall." *And the faster I help them get better, the sooner we can find them a new home.*

"That's very mature of you, dear." Her mom sneaked another bit of cookie dough. "But it makes me feel old to see my thirteen-year-old daughter acting so grown-up. Are you sure you don't want me or your father to handle it?"

"I'll be fine, Mom, really," Ali said. "I'll catch some sleep as soon as these cookies are out of the oven, then set my alarm."

It was after 10:00 when Ali finally got the cookies baked and the kitchen cleaned up. Though she could barely keep her eyes open, she pulled a plate down from the cupboard and put a half dozen cookies on it. Then she filled a glass with ice-cold milk and put everything on a tray.

Ali carried the tray upstairs, placed it in front of Danny's door, and knocked. Surprised to hear him making his way to the door, she hightailed it to her room and closed the door without making a sound. Danny's door creaked open. There was a long pause and she imagined him looking up and down the hallway, wondering who had left the cookies. His door closed with a soft click.

Ali put on pajamas and crawled into bed. Maybe she'd make a special plate of cookies for Jamie and his dad tomorrow. She set the alarm to wake her in a couple of hours, then closed her eyes and quickly drifted off to sleep.

❧

When her alarm went off a while later, Ali sat up in bed and rubbed her eyes. "Ugh!" she muttered, scooting her legs over the side of the bed and fishing in the dark for her barn clothes. She felt like a rag doll as she stood and pulled on her jeans and T-shirt. Why hadn't she let her mom take over this late-night feeding? She grabbed the flashlight off her dresser and went downstairs, the beam of light slicing a through the darkness. Stumbling outside, she made her way to the horse corrals.

Both horses were lying down, but Misty stood and shook the sand from her coat before making her way to the fence. She nickered and extended her nose, pushing her muzzle into Ali's hair.

Ali closed her eyes and breathed in the heady scent of horse. Memories of Max floated through her mind. She reached out her hand and allowed herself, and Misty, one good pat and ear scratch. Better Misty than Wind Dancer.

She gave one bucket to each horse, barely looking at Wind Dancer. Much to Ali's surprise, the gelding gingerly got to his feet and shuffled over to the bucket, pushing his nose down into the hay. He chewed loudly, grinding the hay in his molars and swallowing. He was eating fairly slowly—especially compared to Misty, who had already wolfed down her ration and was begging for more. But he was eating on his own, and that gave Ali a big sense of accomplishment.

She tiptoed back to her room, too tired to even get out of her horse clothes before she fell sound asleep.

Ali woke to the sound of chirping birds. Something was wrong. Sunlight flooded her room. She sat straight up in bed and reached for her alarm clock. It hadn't gone off...because she had forgotten to reset it before falling asleep last night.

She'd slept straight through the last feeding! Ali leaped out of bed and pulled on her jeans and boots. She finger-combed her hair as she ran down the staircase. What would Jamie and Dr. Forrester have to say? She was as bad as Mrs. Marshall!

Her mother sat at the kitchen table. "How'd the late night feedings go?" she asked.

"I'll explain everything in a minute." Ali ran out the back door. How could she have overslept? She should have set her cell phone alarm too.

Ali came to a screeching halt at the horse pen. Both horses stood in big piles of hay—at least two or three flakes from the looks of it.

"Stop! Don't eat that!" She rushed into Wind Dancer's pen

and shooed him away from the hay. Though she was desperate to get the hay away from him, she was also surprised to see he was actually eating it. How much had he consumed already? He was only supposed to get a quarter of a flake and there was ten times that amount on the ground. How long had the horses been eating?

She gathered armloads of alfalfa and chucked it over the fence, then ran to Misty's pen and repeated the procedure. There was much less hay there. Had the mare eaten more, or been fed less?

Who could have done this? Her parents knew better. Ali looked around their property. Could an early riser have seen the skinny horses and tried to do them a favor? If only she knew how much each horse had eaten!

She checked Misty over first. The mare had a big appetite; she had probably consumed more than Wind Dancer had. That would put her in bigger trouble.

She wasn't really sure what symptoms she should look for. The vet had said it would take three to five days for refeeding syndrome to appear. She racked her brain, trying to remember anything else the vet had told her.

She looked at her watch. Dr. Forrester and Jamie were due here any minute. She hoped they weren't late.

Ali slipped into Wind Dancer's pen and looked him over. He seemed about the same as he had last night. Would it make a difference that the horses had missed a feeding before their big meal?

Why didn't I set both alarms? She needed to tell her parents. They might know what to do.

Danny hobbled around the corner. "Did they eat all their hay?" he asked.

"It was *you?*"

Danny tried to coax Wind Dancer over to the fence, seemingly unaware of the anger in his sister's voice. "No one was up yet, and that white mare kept nickering like she wanted to be fed," he said. "They're so skinny; I thought I'd throw them some extra hay."

"Danny…" Ali tried to control her reaction. "Do you know what you've done?"

Danny's smile turned into a confused frown. "I fed the horses," he said. "Isn't that what you've been doing?"

Ali closed her eyes, willing herself not to be sick. Up until last night, Danny had never shown any interest in horses—not even Max. No one had bothered to tell him anything about the limited feeding program of these horses because no one expected him to have anything to do with them.

She took a deep breath. "Danny, you shouldn't have done that. They can't have that much food. They could die!"

He looked stricken, then his cheeks reddened. "I can't seem to do anything right these days!" He tossed his hands in the air. "Why do I even bother to try? I should have never come home!" Her brother lurched away, shoulders slumped.

"Danny…wait!" Why had she spoken so harshly? Danny was already struggling. She shouldn't have blamed him. If she'd only set her alarm. She ran after him.

Danny spun around on his crutches and glared at her. "Don't follow me!"

The words cut Ali to the quick. They were the exact words he had said before she had followed him into the desert on Max.

Ali watched her brother clumsily negotiate the back steps to the house. Why couldn't she have found the right words?

Danny hadn't intended to harm the horses. He thought he was helping.

Danny glanced over his shoulder just before he entered the house. The look on his face broke Ali's heart. She should have kept her mouth shut. Not only had she lost this battle, she'd lost the whole silly war. And worst of all, she'd lost her brother all over again.

Thirteen

ires crunched on the gravel. Dr. Forrester and Jamie had arrived. Ali stared at the house for a few more seconds, willing Danny to reappear, though she knew he wouldn't.

She'd deal with her brother later. For now, she had to focus on how to help the horses. "Mom! Dad!" she yelled. "The vet is here. Can you come help, please?"

Her mom stuck her head out the door. "I'll be there in a minute, dear. Right after I see what's up with your brother."

Why do problems always come in big bunches? She'd have to explain the situation to her parents. But first, she had to tell Jamie and his dad just how badly she'd messed up.

Jamie had a big smile on his face. Ali tried to smile back, but it didn't work. "Is everything okay?" he asked.

Ali took a steadying breath. "We might have a problem," she said. *That's the understatement of the year.*

Dr. Forrester climbed out of the truck. "What kind of problem?"

"It's all my fault," she began. "I did a feeding at 9:00 last night and another a little after 1:00 AM. I was so tired, I forgot to set my alarm for the 5:00 AM feeding. I just woke up. When I came down to feed…"

"And...?" the veterinarian prompted. "Missing a feeding by a few hours isn't good, but it shouldn't cause much of a problem. Is there something else?"

Ali waved her hand at the big pile of hay outside of the corrals. "My brother thought he was helping. He didn't know that the horses were only supposed to get a little bit to eat. I don't know how long or how much they've eaten."

"Can't you ask your brother how much he gave them?" Jamie asked.

Ali shook her head. "Danny's been under a lot of stress since he came home from the war." She stared up at his bedroom window, wondering what he was doing up there. The blinds were tightly closed. "I kind of accused him of harming the horses and he got upset. I don't think he'll talk to anyone for a while. But from what I can tell, he gave them two or three flakes apiece."

Dr. Forrester looked at the pile of loose hay. "From the looks of it, I don't think they could have eaten all that much." He took his stethoscope from his bag and entered Wind Dancer's pen. "We'll just have to figure this out ourselves," he said. "I'll start with this guy since he's in the worst shape."

He listened to Wind Dancer's heartbeat. The gelding stood with his head down and his ears out to the side, a little more alert than he'd been in the previous days, but still not very active.

Ali waited anxiously while the vet moved the instrument around on the horse's belly. "What are you checking for?" she asked.

"Gut sounds," the vet replied. "A horse with a healthy stomach will have a lot of noise going on in there after they've eaten. If you don't get much sound after a meal, that might indicate trouble. I'm also listening to his heart and lungs to see if anything is amiss." He took another few minutes to examine the gelding, then straightened and pulled the stethoscope out of his ears.

Ali's parents joined her at the fence. "What's going on?" her father asked.

"Danny came into the house with a full head of steam and went straight to his bedroom," her mother said. "What happened out here?"

Ali didn't know where to start. Thankfully, Dr. Forrester stepped in. "It looks like Danny didn't know about the feeding instructions. He thought he was helping by giving the horses a big pile of hay."

"Oh, no!" Her mother looked at Ali. "I guess that explains a lot."

"I'll talk to Danny in a bit," Ali's dad said. "He needs a little time to cool off." He turned to the vet. "How are the horses faring?"

Dr. Forrester motioned for Jamie to halter the white mare. "Wind Dancer's heart rate and breathing are a bit lower than I would like," he said. "But he seems to be digesting his food okay. I haven't examined the white mare yet, but I'll have to monitor these horses closely for the next several days to see if they're showing any signs of refeeding syndrome. I'm going to take some blood samples from both of them and see what their electrolyte balance is. That'll tell us what's going on with their organ functions. Their electrolyte levels will drop significantly if they're going into refeeding syndrome. If that happens, we've got big trouble."

"I'm really sorry, Dr. Forrester." Ali hung her head. "This is all my fault."

The veterinarian smiled. "Don't be too hard on yourself, missy. You're taking on a big load of responsibility here with some very sick horses. Even with the best of care and no mistakes, they could still have trouble."

Ali's mom put her arm around Ali's shoulders. "It's mostly our fault, honey. Your father and I shouldn't have let you shoulder so much of this job."

"I know you wanted to handle most of the work yourself," her father said. "But we should have stepped in and insisted that we help you a little more, Ali. We're the parents. We're supposed to know this stuff."

"It's okay." Ali crammed her hands into her jeans pockets and stared at the ground. "You guys are dealing with a lot right now with Danny. I wanted to do most of the work with the horses to help take some of the load off."

"We all should have communicated a little better," her mother said. "Maybe then this wouldn't have happened."

"What if the horses do get sick?" Ali asked.

"We don't have time to worry about the *what-ifs*," the vet said. "Let's concentrate on *what is* and where we go from here."

Ali kept her eyes on the ground and nodded. She didn't want anyone to see the tears that were forming in her eyes.

"Come on, Ali," Jamie said. "My dad is right. Sometimes stuff happens that's out of our control. It's not time to give up. There's still plenty of hope."

"I haven't given up," she said, willing back the tears. "I just hope they're going to be okay."

Dr. Forrester drew a blood sample from each of the horses, then carefully packed the vials for transport. "The labs are normally closed on Sunday," he said. "But a good friend of mine runs the local one, so I'll drop these off as soon as I'm done here. In the meantime, I want to give them some intravenous fluids. We need to make sure they're getting some electrolytes and essential vitamins and minerals back into their system. That'll help keep them from getting refeeding syndrome."

"What do you want me to do?" Ali asked. "How can I help?"

"Yes, Doctor," Ali's mom said. "If there's something that we can all do, please let us know."

"I want you to keep them on the program I gave you," Dr. Forrester said. "Feed small amounts of alfalfa every four hours. Maybe walk them a little bit in their pen if they seem up to it. You can even brush them a bit to make them feel good and improve their circulation. We'll be back in a few hours once we get the results of these tests."

Jamie helped his dad pack up the truck, then waved good-bye as they drove away.

It was going to be a long few hours before they heard from the vet. Hours of wondering if she had caused a catastrophe. She needed to think of other things.

Dr. Forrester had suggested walking the horses or brushing them. Ali frowned. If it helped them get better, maybe she should do it.

"I'll check on Danny," Ali's dad said, heading back to the house.

Ali's mom leaned on the fence rail. "I'll stay out here until your father has had a chance to talk to him." Ali grabbed the brush bucket and handed the new body brush to her mom. "Can you help me groom them? I'll use the curry comb. You can go behind me with the body brush and sweep off all the dirt and hair." She opened the gate to Wind Dancer's pen.

She moved the rubber curry comb in circles across the gelding's coat. Wind Dancer blew through his lips and twitched his ears. He seemed to be enjoying the rub, but he still didn't respond to her like he had her brother.

"So, what exactly happened with you and Danny?" her mother asked.

Ali shrugged. "He was just trying to help, and I came down on him pretty hard," she admitted. "He got mad and stomped off."

"I see." Her mother ran the brush across Wind Dancer's back. "Your brother has had a very hard time adjusting, Ali. I'm sure you've noticed. We've been trying to get him some help, but he doesn't want it. He's a grown man now. We can't force him into anything he doesn't want to do. Your father and I are kind of at our wit's end."

"It doesn't help that he's stubborn as a dang mule," Ali said.

The corners of her mother's mouth lifted a bit and Ali smiled too.

They finished up Wind Dancer and moved to Misty's corral. The mare nudged Ali's shirt when she came near. No doubt about it, Misty was in much better shape than Wind Dancer. The mare nudged her again. Misty definitely wanted to be friends.

"Danny's not the same as when he left," Ali continued. "I knew things were bad, but you and Dad never talked to me about it, so I looked up some stuff on the internet."

Ali looked at Wind Dancer. What was it was about her brother that the horse preferred? She really shouldn't care. He wasn't her horse. But, still, it picked at her. Danny didn't even like horses.

"What did you find out?" her mother asked.

Ali paused with her brush in midair while she tried to form her thoughts. There was no easy way to say it. "I think Danny has PTSD."

Her mother nodded sadly. "Your father and I think so too. But Danny keeps insisting that he's fine."

"There's an organization called the National Center for PTSD." Ali grabbed a comb and concentrated on Misty's mane. "They've got a lot of helpful information. I could show you and Dad where it is on the internet. And the Department of Veterans Affairs has a huge website with all kinds of stuff. There's even a psychologist who wrote a book called *Taming the Fire Within*. She's giving it away for free online to help soldiers with PTSD."

"There's a lot of help out there," her mother agreed. "The problem is getting your brother to seek that help." She rubbed the chain she wore around her neck and stared off into the distance. "I think your brother is...ashamed." She looked Ali in the eye. "I don't know what it's going to take to get him to see that he needs help."

Danny had almost killed them yesterday, all because of a backfire from a car. If that wasn't enough to scare him into seeking help, what would it take? She thought about telling her mom about the incident. She'd promised not to. And she wanted Danny to know he could trust her. But what good was keeping a promise if it didn't help the person it was supposed to protect?

"Ali?" her mother broke into her thoughts. "Is there something bothering you?"

Ali shook her head. "No, I'm just worried about Danny." If things didn't get better soon, she'd tell her mom and dad about the trip to the feed store.

"There's a local branch of the VA here," her mother continued. "Your father and I have decided to attend one of the meetings they hold for families. I guess it's a good place to start. We're finally realizing that this isn't something we can handle by ourselves. Maybe you'd like to go with us?"

"I think that's a really good idea, Mom." Ali tossed the brushes in the bucket and hugged her mother. "We'll find a way to get through to him. We have to. Even if it's tough."

Her mom kissed the top of her head. "I know you've been trying really hard to make your brother feel at home, and it hasn't been easy," she said. "But we'll keep trying. Danny fought for us. Now it's our turn to return the favor."

Her mother opened the gate. "Do you think we should find another person to care for the horses, Ali? Is this too much for us to handle?"

"No!" Ali was surprised by her sudden outburst. "I promised that I would help these horses. School is almost out. I'll have more time then and so will Cara. When they're back in good condition we can talk about finding them another home."

But even as the words came out of her mouth, Ali wondered, if the horses made it through this crisis all right, would she really be able to let them go? She hated to admit it, but try as she might to keep her distance from them, Wind Dancer and Misty were working their way into her heart.

Fourteen

The phone rang as Ali finished her tuna sandwich. Her mother answered it and cupped her hand over the mouthpiece. "It's Dr. Forrester," she whispered. Ali waited anxiously to hear what he had to say.

"Thank you, Doctor; we'll see you in a few minutes." Her mom hung up the phone and turned to her daughter. "The electrolyte levels in both horses have dropped, which isn't good. And Wind Dancer's results showed some other troubles too. Let's go outside and wait for the vet."

Ali pulled on her boots and followed her mom out to the corrals. She had a sick feeling in the pit of her stomach. Misty nickered to them, but Wind Dancer just stood in the corner, his bottom lip drooping. Though they'd just brushed him, his coat still looked dull and lifeless—just like the gelding himself.

Ali spoke softly to Wind Dancer as she ran her fingers through his thin mane. She didn't get the kind of response she was hoping for, but the gelding did rotate his ears once or twice at the sound of her voice.

The day was beginning to warm, and pesky flies started to appear. She made a mental note to pick up a couple of fly masks at the feed store. Ali leaned against the fence and wiped the moisture from her brow. A large whiskered muzzle blew warm breath on her cheek and tickled her ear and she jumped.

"Looks like you've got a friend," her mother observed. "I think Misty likes you. She keeps trying to get your attention. Let's get her water bucket filled before it gets too warm and she needs a cool drink."

"I'll get it, Mom." Ali turned on the hose and crawled through the fence into Misty's pen. "You keep an eye out for the vet." While Ali filled the bucket, Misty bobbed her head and turned to nuzzle her shirt. "You're a lot friendlier than Wind Dancer." She pushed Misty's spotted muzzle away.

Dr. Forrester and Jamie pulled into the drive just as Ali was putting the hose away. She walked out to greet him. "How bad is it?" she asked, chewing her lip nervously.

"It's not as bad as it could be." He pulled out the test results. "Misty's blood work is okay, everything considered, but I'm concerned about Wind Dancer's electrolyte levels. They're dropping pretty significantly, and that's not good. If they go much lower, it will indicate that refeeding syndrome might be setting in. I don't like the looks of his liver function either."

"What does that mean, as far as treatment goes?" Ali's mom asked. "Is there something that can be done?"

The vet walked to the back of his truck and opened the compartment that held all the medicines. "Hold these for me while I get the IV drip." He handed Jamie several small plastic tubes. "Yes," he said to Ali's mom. "There is definitely something we can do to fight this. We need to keep their electrolytes up. The tubes I just handed Jamie are electrolyte paste. It can be given orally. I'll show you how to administer it and give you a dosage schedule before we leave. If we can get the electrolyte levels back up, that might improve the liver function too."

He motioned for Ali to halter Wind Dancer. "I'm going to give them a dose of electrolytes intravenously, along with an antibiotic to start with. Have you tried feeding them since they had that big breakfast?"

"No, sir." Ali slipped the halter over Wind Dancer's head. "You said to feed them every four hours, and it's just a little past that since they last ate."

Jamie picked up Misty's halter. "I'll feed the mare while you're working on Wind Dancer."

"This won't hurt much," Ali said softly to the gelding. She scratched his neck. "It's going to make you better." Wind Dancer cocked his ear slightly. Ali had hoped for a bigger reaction, but for now, that was as good as she was going to get.

The vet brought the IV bag into Wind Dancer's pen. Ali cringed when she saw the size of the needle.

"Just keep rubbing him so he doesn't pay any attention to the needle," Ali's mom said. "Poor Wind Dancer."

"It's not as bad as it looks," Dr. Forrester reassured her. "A horse is a big animal. Their shots are bigger than ours." He turned to Ali. "It's going to take at least ten minutes to administer this drip. It's your job to keep him as still as you can so we don't have to worry about the needle coming out, okay?"

Ali nodded. She stroked the horse's forelock and spoke softly to him. But Wind Dancer acted like she wasn't even there. He barely even flinched when the needle went in. Ali reacted for him, grimacing and turning her head. Misty nickered to her friend, but Wind Dancer just stood there.

"How often will we need to do this?" Ali's mom asked.

"Well, if you guys make sure you feed him that paste, this one IV might do it," Dr. Forrester said. "I don't think he ate that much this morning because his appetite is still off. But his electrolytes are down from what they were yesterday, so something is affecting him. It could just be that he was down so far that even this small amount of food is causing problems. We've got to do everything we can to reverse that trend. We'll continue on with the feedings as usual, but we'll need to keep giving him extra electrolytes."

When they were done with the treatment, Jamie brought in the gelding's feed. "Here, try to get him to eat some of this."

Ali shook her head and pushed the bucket back to him. "Could you please do it this time?" she asked. "You're really good at getting Wind Dancer to eat. We can't take any chances. I'll stand here and hold him while you try."

Jamie nodded and tucked some alfalfa into Wind Dancer's mouth.

Ali spoke to Wind Dancer. "You've got to eat some of this and get your strength up," She rubbed his neck. "You need to be strong like your stablemate. Misty is getting better by the hour. You want to be able to buck and play with her again, right?"

"Keep talking," Doctor Forrester said. "He's starting to eat. I think he likes the sound of your voice."

That lifted Ali's spirits. The more Wind Dancer chewed, the better she felt.

Jamie managed to get Wind Dancer to eat half his ration of alfalfa. "I was hoping his appetite would be a little better," he said as he hung the bucket on the fence. "But at least he's still eating."

Dr. Forrester handed Ali and her mom some of the tubes.

"You need to follow my instructions carefully," he said. "Too many electrolytes can cause just as much trouble as too few. Move the plunger to this mark." He showed Ali the dosage. "You can give it to them at feed time. Just insert the tube into the side of their mouths—like you do when you worm a horse—and deposit it on their tongues. They're too weak to fight, so you shouldn't have any trouble giving the dosage. I'll be back in the morning to take another blood sample."

"How will we know if he's getting worse?" Ali's mom asked. "Are there any symptoms that we should look for?"

"Yes," the vet said. "If his electrolytes start to drop again, his muscles will get weak. You might see him stumble or maybe lie down and not be able to get up. If he's really bad, he might even have a seizure. If you see *any* of these symptoms, call me immediately."

"Thank you, Doctor. We'll help Ali keep watch tonight." She turned to her daughter. "I'd better write all of this down to make sure I have all the details we need. Your father and I will take over your feeding duties while you're in school tomorrow."

Ali had forgotten all about school. The horses were her responsibility. She didn't want to leave them when Wind Dancer was this bad. "I haven't missed any school this year, Mom. And I'm getting good grades. Can I please stay home tomorrow?"

"I could bring you your assignments, if your teachers are okay with it," Jamie volunteered.

Ali's dad joined them. From his expression, he hadn't had much success with Danny. "How's it look, Doc?" he asked. "Are they going to be okay?"

Dr. Forrester picked up his medical bag. "We're going to have to watch them closely, but I believe we can get a handle on it. I've given your wife and daughter their instructions. I have faith that these horses are in good hands." He smiled at Ali and her mom. "If anything comes up, no matter what time, just give me a call and I'll come over immediately."

Ali thanked Jamie and Dr. Forrester, and as they packed up, she went into the house with her parents. "Please, Mom and Dad?" she begged. "Please let me stay home from school tomorrow. The horses really need me and I've got to make up for what happened this morning when I overslept. Besides," she added, "you two never had horses before we got Max. I don't mean any disrespect...but I'm kind of the only real horse person here. I might be able to see important changes in their behavior quicker than you would."

Ali's dad chuckled. "Hey, are you trying to say you have more horse sense than we do?"

Ali smiled. "Yeah, I guess I am," she teased him back. "I just couldn't think of a good way to put it."

"Okay, as long as it's all right with your mother, and as long as you get your homework done," her dad relented. "Your mother and I will do the just-before-dawn feeding so you can sleep in a bit."

"Can I ask one more favor?" Ali bit her bottom lip, knowing she was pushing the envelope. "Could I sleep outside tonight? That way I don't have to keep tromping up and down the stairs."

"I don't know, Ali," Mrs. McCormick said. "You know we've got coyotes here."

"Cara and I have slept outside in the tent before," Ali pointed out. "We didn't have any trouble. Or you could park the truck right next to the corrals and I could sleep inside it. Then I could blast the horn if something happens." She pulled a bottle of water out of the refrigerator. "Dr. Forrester says I need to keep a really close eye on the horses for the next few days. I can do it better if I'm out there with them."

Her dad looked to his wife. "She has a point. She *has* spent the night in the tent in the backyard. I'll let you make the call on this one."

Her mother thought for a few moments, then answered. "Danny's window is right there overlooking where you'll be staying," she said. "He'd hear you immediately if something happened."

"So, does that mean yes?" Ali asked.

"Oh, I suppose," her mother said. "Your father and I will check in on you throughout the night. We'll be there if you need help."

"Thanks, Mom and Dad!" Ali ran to her room to finish her homework. Maybe Cara could pick it up from her in the morning and take it to school.

Ali made her way downstairs for dinner. She heard Danny coming just as she sat down. The repeated sound of his crutch thumping on the floor was followed by his remaining foot hitting the tiles. It was a slow, labored cadence.

"Is it okay if I eat my dinner in my room tonight?" he asked, not even looking at Ali. "I'm not feeling that great, and one of my buddies from Afghanistan is on Skype. He's not online very often and I'd really like to see how he's doing over there, along with the rest of the unit."

"Is that Jeff, the boy from Nebraska?" their mother asked.

"Yeah." Danny looked over the roast beef, broccoli, and sweet potato casserole that were already on the table.

Their mom and dad shared a glance. "I think that will

probably be okay for tonight, son." Their dad grabbed Danny's dinner plate and began filling it with food.

"I'll follow you up with your plate and a glass of milk. But Danny?" Their mom gave him one of her I-mean-it stares. "No more missed dinners unless you are truly ill. Understand?"

Danny nodded, then turned and made his way back up the stairs. Ali followed him with her eyes. Did he really intend to talk to his friend in Afghanistan, or did he just not want to sit at the table with her? She pushed the broccoli around on her plate, promising herself that next time she'd think first before opening her mouth.

"Ali, you've only got a few days before you're out for the summer," her mother said. "So no more talk about missing school after tomorrow, kiddo. Your father and I will take over during the day."

Ali grinned. "All right. Thanks for tomorrow." She started clearing the table, but her mom shooed her out of the kitchen. "You go take care of those horses."

In the corral, Ali prepared the feed buckets. Once again Misty ate all her food and begged for more. But Wind Dancer ate less than he had earlier.

"Come on, boy," Ali murmured. "You've got to eat some more so you can get better." She fetched the electrolyte paste she was supposed to administer. "I've got something here that's going to help you."

Misty nickered like she thought Ali had a treat for them. "I'm sorry, girl." Too bad she couldn't give the mare some tidbit—a piece of apple or a small bit of grain, especially since the mare seemed to be doing so much better than her stablemate.

Misty tossed her head a couple of times and Ali felt a tug

on her heartstrings. If she didn't get these horses better and find a new owner for them soon, she was going to be in deep trouble. "I'm sorry, girl, but I really can't," Ali said, turning away.

She concentrated on giving the electrolytes to Wind Dancer. "Here we go," she said as she inserted the tube in the corner of his mouth. Wind Dancer wrinkled his nostrils like he didn't really like the taste, but he swallowed several times, then accepted a few small bites of alfalfa from her palm. "That's it, big guy. You're getting the hang of it."

Ali put the buckets away and went inside to gather her sleeping bag, pillow, and cell phone. If only it wasn't a school night, Cara could have stayed with her.

She hauled all of her things down to the truck. Her mom lit the way with a flashlight and made sure she was secure in the front seat. "I packed you a bag of popcorn and a soda," she said. "Are you sure you're going to be okay out here?"

"Come on, Mom. I'm in my own backyard. You guys are right there in the house. I've got my cell phone. I'll call if I need to. Don't worry. Everything is going to be fine."

But at midnight, Wind Dancer only ate a couple handfuls of feed, leaving the rest of the bucket untouched. Ali tried to ignore the cold feeling in the pit of her stomach, but it wouldn't go away. A diminished appetite in an already sick animal wasn't a good sign. But Wind Dancer was still able to stand and shuffle around. There was no sign of the muscle fatigue or seizures that Dr. Forrester had warned her about.

"Why won't you get better?" she whispered as she stroked the gelding's rough coat. His body felt warm in the cool night air.

"I've got to get these buckets set up for your next meal," she told Wind Dancer. She picked up the plastic pails and set them outside the corral.

The moon had traveled across the night sky, lighting the corrals and shining down on the horses. Misty's white coat reflected the pale beams, making her easier to see. With his black coat, Wind Dancer disappeared into the shadows, with only the white blanket on his rump showing.

Misty stood near the dividing fence, bobbing her head and nickering. Ali took a moment to pet her before returning to the truck to catch a few more hours of sleep. If Wind Dancer's appetite didn't improve by the next feeding, she'd have to call Dr. Forrester.

Ali crawled into the truck and snuggled down deep in her sleeping bag. It still got a little chilly at night, but she needed to keep the truck window cracked so she could hear the horses. She texted her parents, letting them know she was okay, then set the alarm to wake her up in another four hours.

As she lay on the front seat of the truck looking out at the stars, Ali listened to the sounds of the night. Misty shuffled around in her pen looking for any stray bits of hay she might have dropped. Wind Dancer grunted as he lay down in his corral and stretched out for some sleep.

Far up in the mountains, the coyotes yipped. Maybe they'd found a fat rabbit to chase. The coyote calls set off a chorus of neighborhood dogs, leaving Ali to wonder if she'd ever be able to fall asleep. Did the noise disturb the horses the way it did her?

After a while her eyelids grew heavy and she began to drift off. A train whistle blew in the distance. It sounded so forlorn, echoing the sadness she felt inside. No matter how hard they all tried, Wind Dancer might slip away from them anyway.

Around 2:00 AM, Ali was woken by the sound of shoes crunching on gravel. She peeked out the truck window, expecting her mom or dad, but it was her brother.

Danny stood outside Wind Dancer's corral. "Come here, boy." He held out his palm, coaxing the Appaloosa over. He called softly to the gelding several times and Wind Dancer finally stood up and ambled over.

"That a boy." Danny stuck his hand through the fencing and rubbed the white star between the gelding's eyes. He put out his palm again and Wind Dancer took something from him. Ali could hear the gelding slowly munching the treat. Was it carrots? Sugar cubes? He probably wasn't supposed to have either of those. Should she say something to Danny? She pictured how his face fell when she yelled at him about feeding Wind Dancer too much before.

She listened to Wind Dancer crunch another treat. If the horse would eat for Danny, she should encourage it. She tried not to feel jealous that Wind Dancer wouldn't eat so easily for her. Her goal was to get the horses better and find them a new home, right?

She shifted uncomfortably in her sleeping bag. Did Danny even know she was out here?

"Why aren't you eating your hay?" Danny asked Wind Dancer. "You need to get your strength back." Danny was quiet for a long time.

"What are we going to do, old boy?" Danny's voice cracked. "You got a raw deal here. Your life is pretty messed up. Same with me." He was quiet for a minute. "I went away to war and my world turned upside down, but everything here kept marching on just the same. My friends went to school, went to parties, got married, had babies...they left me behind."

There was a long stretch of silence and Ali wondered if her brother had gone. She was about to look out the truck window when he spoke again.

"Neither one of us seems to be doing very well in this ol' world. What's going to become of us?"

She peeked out the window and watched as he scratched Wind Dancer's ears. Danny lowered his forehead until it touched the gelding's. He stood that way for a long time, then Ali heard both the horse and her brother sigh.

Fifteen

It seemed like only a few minutes had passed when the alarm on Ali's cell phone sounded. It was just before dawn and the early morning chill made her shiver. She slipped out of her sleeping bag, pulled on her boots and a light-weight jacket, and stepped out of the truck.

Misty nickered for her breakfast, but Wind Dancer was lying down again. He seemed to be sleeping. Ali watched him nervously as she grabbed the feed buckets and hung Misty's on the fence post. The mare needed no encouragement to eat.

Ali carried the other bucket into Wind Dancer's pen. To her surprise, he rose quickly to his feet and shook himself from head to tail. He looked a little stronger. "Well, look at you," she said as she walked around the gelding, taking note of his appearance in the pre-dawn haze.

His ears were still flopped out to the side like they'd been since he'd first arrived. Though he didn't seem all that alert, Ali sensed an improvement in his outlook. She lifted her hand and snapped her fingers to check for a reaction. Wind Dancer's ears twitched at the sound. "Good boy," she said. Maybe the electrolytes and antibiotics were starting to work? Or maybe it was Danny's visit?

She offered the bucket of hay to Wind Dancer. He sniffed the alfalfa and pushed it around with his nose, but he didn't appear to be interested in eating it. A small patch of light crept over the mountains as Ali waited patiently for the gelding to eat.

A lone meadowlark sang in the desert beyond their house; it was soon joined by desert scrub jays and other birds. A jackrabbit sprang from its hiding place beneath a peach bush and sprinted across the sand.

Ali breathed in the fresh smell of sagebrush. It was kind of cool being up this time of day and seeing the desert come to life. She reached out to straighten Wind Dancer's forelock and rub the star on his forehead.

Something at the far end of the pen caught Ali's eye. She put down the alfalfa bucket and went to see what it was. Bending down, she found a few tidbits of carrot. Danny must have left them. She glanced back at Wind Dancer. He still showed little interest in his morning feed. "Here, boy." She held the goodies out for him to sniff. The gelding's ears came forward a little, but he ignored the treats.

Ali picked up the bucket of hay and put it under his nose, Wind Dancer lipped it, but he didn't take a bite. She took some of the soft leaves and gently pushed them into his mouth. The gelding held them for a moment, then slowly began to grind the food.

Ali picked up the bucket and offered him some more alfalfa. "That's a good boy." Ali tilted the bucket to make it easier for him to eat. She stood patiently while the gelding picked through the bucket. When he was almost to the bottom of the feed pail, he stopped eating and pushed the hay away.

She couldn't keep the smile off of her face. The horses weren't out of danger yet, but Misty was definitely on the way, and Wind Dancer was showing promise for the first time.

She fed Misty a piece of carrot and put the buckets away. This time, she would have good news to report to Dr. Forrester.

Ali stretched her stiff muscles. Her warm bed was calling to her. Maybe she could squeeze in a few hours of good sleep before the vet arrived?

Ali heard a noise from the other side of the barn, near the chicken pen. She decided to check it out and feed the chicks before she went inside. The sun was almost up.

She turned the corner and stopped dead in her tracks. Danny sat in the middle of the chicken coop with both chicks nestled in his lap. His head was bowed and he didn't look up as she approached. Was he asleep? Had he been here since he left the horses last night?

"Danny?" She crept forward slowly, remembering what happened the last time she had surprised him when he was sleeping. Her brother's shoulders were shaking. Was he crying? A knot formed in the pit of her stomach. "Danny?"

He looked up and Ali could see the tracks of tears on his face. He stared through her like she was invisible.

"Danny!" Ali opened the door to the pen and ran to her brother. The chicks scattered. "Danny, what's wrong?" She dropped to her knees, grabbed his shoulders, and forced him to look at her.

Danny blinked. "I don't know what's wrong." He sounded childlike—not like a grown man who had been to war. "Something's wrong and I don't know what it is. I can't even help myself." He spread his hands in bewilderment. "What am I going to do, sis? I don't know what I'm going to do. *Tell me what I'm supposed to do.*"

Danny folded inward, his chin resting on his chest. She could feel his shoulders tremble. Several tears fell onto his lap. She couldn't tell if they were Danny's or hers.

The weight of her brother's sadness pressed down upon her. Danny had always been a rough-and-tumble kind of guy. Her strong big brother. What should she say to him? How could she make it better?

Ali did the only thing she could think of. She leaned forward and hugged him. "Shhhh," she whispered. "It's going to be okay, Danny. We'll figure this out…all of us. You, me, Mom, and Dad. We're here for you."

Danny ran his sleeve across his eyes then returned the hug, holding on tight, as if Ali was the only thing keeping him anchored to the earth.

Ali held her brother, making comforting noises and patting his back while Danny sobbed. She had to be strong. Strong for her brother, because right now he didn't have the strength to fight for himself.

One of the little chicks scrambled back onto his lap. Danny sniffed and lifted his head. His eyes were almost swollen shut; he looked like he'd been in a fight. "Well…," he said. "At least the chickens still like me."

Then he burst out laughing. "What a sorry excuse for a soldier I am," Danny said, "blubbering all over my little sister like I've lost my mind." He set Ali and the chick aside and reached for his crutches, working his way up to stand. "Ali, don't tell—"

Ali tweaked his arm before he could get the rest of the sentence out. "No, Danny, I'm *not* going to promise not to tell

Mom and Dad! You can't pretend this didn't happen!" She flung her arm out to indicate him, the chicken pen where he'd slept, the chicks, the breakdown he'd just had.

She was so mad, her voice shook as she hollered. "You're not going to brush this aside like you usually do!" She was sure that the neighbors could hear every word, but she didn't care. "This scared the heck out of me, Danny. And it should have scared you too." She put her hands on her hips and glared at him. "I heard you talking to Wind Dancer last night. I was sleeping in the truck."

Danny glared at her, but said nothing.

Ali thought about all that had happened since her brother had returned. All the signs were there: the moodiness, the anger, the solitude, the depression.

"Danny, you've got to talk to us about this," Ali insisted. "You need help."

"I don't have to talk about anything." Danny turned to leave and the chicks scattered.

Ali jumped up and ran to the pen's door. She slammed it closed. "I know I'm younger than you and smaller than you, but you're not getting out of this pen until we talk."

Danny tilted his head as if weighing her words. He backed up, leaning against the chicken coop, and crossed his arms. "Fine. Go ahead and talk."

Good, Ali thought, but now she had to figure out what to say to make Danny listen. "I've been reading a lot of things on the internet—"

"Don't believe everything you see online," he snapped.

Maybe Ali should just lock him in the pen and run and get her mom and dad. What chance did she have of convincing him of anything?

Ali looked at her brother; *really* looked at him. Danny was twenty years old. He was missing part of a leg and his body was covered with scars from flying shrapnel. And then there were the scars she couldn't see. The ones on the inside.

She began to shake. "This is all my fault," Ali said. "If I hadn't followed you that day, Max wouldn't have thrown me and I wouldn't have broken my arm. Max wouldn't have died and you wouldn't have been sent off to the Army. You'd still have your leg and everything would be fine."

"Don't say that, Ali!" Danny pushed off of the chicken coop and balanced on his crutches. "None of this is your fault."

"Yes it is!" she sputtered between choking breaths. "It's *all* my fault, the stuff that happened to you. You were sent away because of *me.*"

"That's not true." Danny took a few hobbling steps toward her. "I chose to join the Army. Mom and Dad didn't send me. I could see I was heading down a bad path." He moved a little closer. "This...," he said, indicating his leg. "This is the fault of the men who set that bomb; not yours, not mine, not anyone else's."

Danny lifted Ali's chin. "Look at me, sis. None of my problems have to do with you."

Ali jerked her chin away. "Yes they do!" She took a step back. "It's my fault, and now I can't get through to you. I can't make you understand that you need help."

He stared at her without saying a word, and that made Ali even madder. "You're so stubborn!" She kicked at the dirt in the chicken pen.

Danny reached for her, but Ali pushed him away, almost knocking him over. "Danny!" she cried as she reached out to steady him.

Danny started laughing.

"What are you laughing at?"

"*Us.* That's what I'm laughing about." He shook his head. "Look at us two knot heads out here barking at each other and getting madder by the second."

The fight went out of her. "You've been so angry since you've come home," she whispered. "I want you to get better and I don't know how to make you get help."

"I understand, sis." Danny hobbled forward and hugged Ali to his chest. "I got the message this time. Let's get on up to the house. We'll sit down with Mom and Dad and talk."

"You really mean it?"

"I can't promise you anything," Danny said. "It's going to be hard for me, and I'm not sure I agree with your assessment. But maybe it's worth looking into PTSD."

Ali opened the gate to the chicken pen and held it for her brother.

"Would you really have locked us in here?"

"Yup." Ali closed the door behind them and followed her brother up to the house. "I'm glad I didn't, though. That would have been kind of hard to explain to Mom and Dad."

Danny glanced at her as they approached the back porch. "Oh, and Ali…maybe you—"

"Don't you dare ask me not tell Mom and Dad about this, Danny. It's too important." She reached out her hand to help him up the steps.

"I know," Danny said.

Sixteen

If either of their parents noticed Ali and Danny's tear-stained faces and puffy eyes, neither said a word.

"Mom, Dad, we all need to talk." Ali pulled out a chair at the kitchen table for Danny, then one for herself. Her heart was hammering in her chest.

"Let me call work and tell them I'm going to be late," their dad said. He grabbed the coffeepot and set it in the middle of the table.

Danny stared at his hands; clearly he wasn't going to be any help. Ali cleared her throat. "Danny has decided that it might be time to make a few changes."

Danny's eyebrows rose at that one.

"Is that true, son?" their mom asked. "What kind of changes are we talking about?"

Danny stared at his hands a bit longer, then looked up. "Ali helped me realize I've been pretty withdrawn here lately. I don't think I realized how much I've disrupted everyone else's lives." He picked at his fingers a bit, then continued. "I'm not willing to admit that I have PTSD or anything just yet, but maybe I *should* talk to someone. Maybe we could all go together."

Ali's mom exhaled and reached across the table to take Danny's hand. "I'm very happy to hear that."

"That's very commendable, Danny," their father said. "I'll get a hold of the VA today and see what they have to offer in the way of family counseling."

Danny poured himself a cup of coffee and the family settled in for a long talk.

By the end of an hour, they'd covered a lot of territory. Ali wasn't sure they'd settled much, but Danny had agreed to consider some ideas, including going back into physical therapy with his new prosthetic and maybe contacting the Wounded Warrior Project. He still wasn't willing to admit he had PTSD, but he agreed to speak to the Veteran's Administration about it.

Ali yawned. "It'll be time to feed the horses again in another hour," she said. "And Dr. Forrester will be here soon. I'll wait up for him."

"Oh no you don't, young lady." Her mother pointed her toward the stairs. "I'll do the feeding and handle the veterinarian. You and Danny get to bed and get some sleep. You've both had a long night."

Danny waved her off. "I'll help you with this feeding, Mom," he volunteered. "You can show me what they're supposed to eat. Ali, you go to bed. Mom can handle the vet. I'll eat in a bit and go to bed after that."

Ali was too tired to argue. Wind Dancer would eat better with Danny holding the bucket. This time she didn't feel even a bit of jealousy. She kissed her mom and dad, hugged Danny, and trudged up the stairs. Boy, would she have a lot to tell Cara when school got out!

Ali washed up and changed into her pajamas. It felt strange going to bed with the sun shining. She crawled between the clean sheets and hugged her pillow. Her eyelids drooped, but she fought to keep them open. She wondered what the vet would think about the small improvement in the horses. But, try as she might, Ali couldn't fight sleep.

Ali awoke to the sound of one of the horses whinnying and carrying on. It was still daylight, but she could tell that many hours had passed. Ali heard hoofbeats coming up the driveway and reached for her clothes. Cara had arrived.

The screen door banged as she came down the steps. Danny's voice rang out. "He's gone!"

"Who's gone?" she asked. *The vet? Jamie?*

"Wind Dancer!" Danny looked stricken. "Your horse is gone, Ali."

Misty neighed again. Now Ali knew why the mare had put up such a fuss. Her stablemate was gone! "How can he be gone? He can barely shuffle around his pen. How did he get loose?" Had she forgotten to close the gate?

"I was the last one to feed them." Danny held the door open for her, and followed her down the steps. "I...I'm so sorry. I think maybe I accidentally left the gate unlocked."

"Don't worry," she reassured Danny. "Wind Dancer couldn't have gone very far."

Danny tried to keep up with her, but his prosthetic was slowing him down. "He seemed to be feeling a little better.

He finished off the entire bucket of alfalfa and the doc gave him more of those electrolytes and antibiotics."

"What's up?" Cara asked as she swung down from the saddle and looked around the corrals. "Where's Wind Dancer?"

"We think his gate was accidentally left open." Ali patted Misty to calm her down. "Easy, girl, we're going to find your friend." She looked to Danny. "Where's Mom?"

"She's checking the barn and nearby houses to see if he went there," Danny said.

Ali eyed the open desert behind their house. That was where she would go if she were a horse looking to be free.

Evening was fast approaching. They had to find Wind Dancer before it got dark. Meanwhile, if he filled up on wild desert grass, he'd end up with refeeding syndrome for sure. And what about coyotes? If Wind Dancer fell and didn't have the strength to get up...

"Cara, can I borrow Dumpling?" Ali asked.

Cara's brows rose. "I thought you didn't ride anymore?"

"I'm about to start," Ali said. "I'll be back down as soon as I change into my boots. Can you put Wind Dancer's halter in your saddlebag, please? I'm going to find him and bring him home."

Danny caught her by the arm as she hurried past. "You can't go out there, sis. It'll be dark soon. There's no way Mom and Dad would let you go."

"Mom and Dad aren't here." She shook off his hand. "I have to go, Danny. I've got to find Wind Dancer before something happens!"

Danny pressed his lips into a hard line. "It's not safe for you to be out in the desert after dark, Ali."

"You're not the boss of me!" Ali shouted. "We're wasting time. And you can't do it, so just let me go." She saw the hurt look on his face and instantly regretted her words. "I...I'm sorry, Danny. I didn't mean..."

He nodded his head toward the house. "Just get your boots and go."

Ali hesitated, but she knew there was nothing she could say to make the situation better. She ran to the house. Inside, she grabbed a light windbreaker and some licorice vines, in case she was gone for a while. She hurried back to the corrals. Cara stood alone, shielding her eyes as she stared out into the desert.

"Where's Dumpling?" Ali asked.

"Out there." Cara pointed to a small speck in the desert.

"Dumpling ran away too?"

"No, your brother is riding him. He's gone after Wind Dancer."

"What?" Ali cried. "Danny can't ride. He's going to get hurt. We've got to go get him."

Ali's mom joined them. "That's Danny out there on Dumpling?" She put a hand on her daughter's shoulder and sighed. "Let him go, Ali. Wind Dancer needs to be brought home. And this might be something your brother needs to do."

Her mother was right. Besides, what could she do? It's not like she could go after him on foot, and Misty wasn't strong enough to be ridden yet. "We've got to call Dr. Forrester," Ali said. "Even if Danny finds him, Wind Dancer might be in really bad shape."

"I'll call the vet and your father," her mother said. She started toward the house.

"And I'll call my mom," Cara said. "I need to let her know I'm going to be here for a while. I want to make sure Danny and Wind Dancer make it back okay."

Ali nodded.

"Ali, Dumpling's a good horse. He'll get them both home safely. And your brother is stubborn as anything. If anyone can do this, he can."

Ali starred out across the desert. What in the world made Danny climb on a horse and take off across the desert just before dark? He'd never really ridden before, and he was wearing his prosthetic. She hoped he knew what he was doing.

Ali's mom returned from the house. "Your dad is almost home, and Doctor Forrester will be here shortly. He'll give Wind Dancer a complete examination when Danny brings him home.

A few minutes later, Ali's dad pulled into the driveway and stopped in a cloud of dust. "Any word?" he said as he got out of the car. "How long has he been gone?"

"Almost an hour." Ali's mom fiddled with the bracelet on her wrist, spinning it round and round.

"I'll call Search and Rescue and put them on alert," her father said as he took out his cell phone.

Misty continued to pace back and forth on the fence line, stopping occasionally to look out over the desert and call to her friend. "Easy, girl," Ali soothed. "They'll all come home safe in a bit."

"Danny's going to be okay," Ali's dad said when he joined them after making the phone call. "That boy's a survivor."

They stood in a row, staring out into the desert. Another thirty minutes passed. A small plane flew over, heading into the desert. "That might be the Search and Rescue crew," Ali's dad said. "If Danny makes it back okay—and I'm sure he will—Wind Dancer may not have the strength to come with him."

Ali's legs grew weak. Did he mean that Wind Dancer might not make it out alive? Of course, that was a distinct possibility. Wind Dancer was in pretty bad shape. How could he have traveled so far from the corral in his condition?

And what about Danny? Her brother struggled to walk across the living room with his new prosthetic. And he wasn't a horseman. What if Dumpling managed to unseat him? Even if Danny caught up with Wind Dancer, how would he be able to maneuver without his cane or crutches?

Dr. Forrester and Jamie arrived a few minutes later. Jamie gave Ali a quick hug. "It's going to be okay. Your brother is a pretty tough cookie from what I hear. He'll be back with that ol' horse in tow before you know it."

Ali attempted a smile. "Thanks."

Dr. Forrester pulled out a couple of folding chairs and offered them to her parents. "I spoke to the Search and Rescue team a few minutes ago. They sent up a plane, but the pilot didn't see anything from the air."

Ali's mom sucked in her breath.

"Now, just a minute, folks," the veterinarian said. "That doesn't necessarily mean anything bad. There's a lot of territory to cover. Your son could have been in one of the canyons or in a long shadow when the pilot went over."

Ali's dad ran his hand through his hair. "I think maybe it's time to get the ground team involved," he said. "It's getting close to sunset. We need to get Danny home." He glanced at Ali. "And Wind Dancer too."

Misty pawed the ground of her corral and snorted. Ali went to the mare, trying to calm her. Misty put her head over Ali's shoulder, and the mare's weight on her felt solid, safe.

Misty let out a loud whinny that nearly pierced Ali's

eardrum. The cry was answered by another horse out in the desert.

"It's got to be Danny!" Ali patted Misty, then climbed to the top rail of the corral to look. She couldn't see them yet, but Misty knew they were coming. They all rushed out from the corrals to the edge of the desert to wait.

Soon Ali could make out the silhouette of a horse and rider, with another horse trailing behind. It was hard to wait patiently while the three of them slowly wound their way through the sagebrush.

At last Danny rode into the yard on Dumpling. He looked tired and strained, but he managed a small smile as he handed the black Appaloosa's lead off to Ali. "I believe this belongs to you."

Wind Dancer looked like he was ready to drop, but he seemed somewhat aware of his surroundings. He nickered softly to Misty and she returned the greeting enthusiastically. Ali took the lead rope, her hands shaking. Her mom and dad helped Danny down and Cara led Dumpling to an empty pen to remove his saddle and bridle.

When Danny was steady on the ground again, Ali hugged him with all her might. She gave Wind Dancer's lead rope back to him. "Danny, I think this horse belongs to *you.*"

"But he's a perfect replacement for Max," Danny said. "You loved that pony, and Wind Dancer looks just like him."

Ali patted the horse affectionately and kissed him on the end of his nose. "There will never be another Max," she said. Misty leaned over the fence and nuzzled her hair. "But it does seem that there's a certain white mare that needs a new owner."

Their mom clapped her hands together.

Ali smiled and scratched Misty on the neck. "Wind Dancer needs you, Danny. And I think you need him too."

"I had a lot of time to think about things while I was out there by myself," Danny admitted. He held Wind Dancer while the vet examined him. "I've thought through the things we talked about this morning. I think I'm ready to talk to somebody about everything that's been going on. PTSD included. I want to get my life back in order."

Wind Dancer nickered. Danny patted him affectionately. "I'm going to need a job so I can support this beast and all the food he's going to eat. I want to get him back into shape so I can learn how to ride him correctly." He rubbed his backside. "I smacked the saddle pretty hard while I was riding Dumpling. I'm pretty sure I wasn't doing it right."

Ali laughed.

"And next time, sis," Danny added, "when you ask if you can follow me out into the desert, I'll say yes."

Ali hugged her brother.

For the first time in a long time, she felt like things really were going to work out. Danny was going to get the help he needed, and they had two great new horses as well.

She watched proudly as Danny walked Wind Dancer into his pen. The gelding was so tired he could barely make it, but he managed to nuzzle her brother's shoulder as he was taking off his halter.

Ali climbed the fence to join Cara. She pulled the licorice from her pocket and gave Cara a piece. "It's going to feel good to be a horse girl again."

"Hmmm. Maybe we can ask a certain boy to join us for a ride when your horses are ready to go?" Cara asked.

"Well, sure," Ali said with a smile. "It's going to be a long road to recovery, and a lot of hard work before these horses will be ready for that, but I can't wait!"

Ali and Cara lifted their pieces of licorice high in the air and crossed them in salute.

"To new beginnings," Cara said.

"To new beginnings," Ali agreed.

Author's Note

Post-traumatic Stress Disorder

Many of our soldiers are returning from war with Post-traumatic Stress Disorder, or PTSD. Most of them will recover over time, but for some, the symptoms won't go away and might even become worse.

For those seeking additional information on this disorder, here is a list of places that offer help and insight:

Mayo Clinic
www.mayoclinic.com/health/post-traumatic-stress-disorder/DS00246

Military.com
www.military.com

National Center for PTSD
www.ptsd.va.gov

National Institute of Mental Health
www.nimh.nih.gov/health/topics/post-traumatic-stress-disorder-ptsd/index.shtml

U.S. Department of Veterans Affairs
www.va.gov

Veterans' Crisis Line
(800) 273-8255

Taming the Fire Within by Dr. Anne Freund
www.tamingthefirewithin.com

Wounded Warrior Project
www.woundedwarriorproject.org

About the author

CHRIS PLATT has been riding horses since she was two years old. At the age of sixteen, she earned her first gallop license at a racetrack in Salem, Oregon. Several years later, she became one of the first female jockeys in that state. Chris has also trained Arabian endurance horses and driven draft horses.

After earning a journalism degree from the University of Nevada in Reno, she decided to combine her love of horses and writing. She is the author of several books, including ASTRA, MOON SHADOW, STAR GAZER, STORM CHASER, and WILLOW KING.

Platt lives in Nevada with her husband, four horses, two cats, and a parrot.

www.chrisplattbooks.com

HORSE BOOKS

from Chris Platt

ASTRA
HC: 978-1-56145-541-6

Forbidden to ride again after her mother's death,
Lily dreams of becoming a great endurance rider.

"...a quick and enjoyable read." —*School Library Journal*

MOON SHADOW
HC: 978-1-56145-382-5 / PB: 978-1-56145-546-1

Callie's love for a beautiful Mustang mare fuels her fierce determination
to save the life—against all odds—of the wild horse's orphaned filly.

"...a heartwarming, wish-come-true story." —*School Library Journal*

STAR GAZER
HC: 978-1-56145-596-6

Jordan is thrilled when she wins a draft horse at an auction, but her joy is short-lived when she
learns that Star Gazer, once the winner of many log pulling contests, is lame and depressed due
to years of neglect. Can Jordan help Star Gazer get his health and confidence back?

"...the story moves at a steady clip..." —*Kirkus Reviews*

STORM CHASER
HC: 978-1-56145-496-9

Jessica goes behind her father's back to work with the wild Storm Chaser. But after an
unexpected disaster at the ranch, going against the rules brings a heavy price...

"Lovely horse details, fine characterization and a real sense of family combine
to make an excellent book..." —*Kirkus Reviews*

WILLOW KING
PB: 978-1-56145-549-2

When a foal is born with legs too crooked to race, his owner orders him destroyed.
But Katie can't bear to let this happen, so she comes up with a plan to save him.

"Horse-crazy readers will find themselves immersed in the racing world,
and will root for Willow King and for Katie all the way." —*Kirkus Reviews*

PEACHTREE PUBLISHERS
www.peachtree-online.com
(800) 241-0113 • (404) 876-8761